fə

THE MADNESS

NARCÍS OLLER

TRANSLATION BY DOUGLAS SUTTLE

INTRODUCTION BY ANDREW DOWLING

FUM D'ESTAMPA PRESS LTD.

LONDON - BARCELONA

This translation has been published in Great Britain
by Fum d'Estampa Press Limited 2020

001

The moral right of the author and translator has been asserted
Set in Minion Pro

Printed and bound by TJ International Ltd, Padstow, Cornwall
A CIP catalogue record for this book is available from the British Library

ISBN: 978-1-9162939-3-9

Series design by 'el mestre' Rai Benach

This work was translated with the help of a grant from the Institut Ramon Llull.

Catalan Language and Culture

FUM D'ESTAMPA PRESS

CONTENTS

INTRODUCTION
BY ANDREW DOWLING

The Madness (La bogeria) by Narcís Oller (1846-1930), which was first
published in 1899, focuses on the gradual then abrupt descent into
madness of an individual named Daniel Serrallonga. Daniel lives in
an imagined town called Vilaniu and is an engineer and landowner.
The Madness is set between 1868 and 1883, with references to
developments in the 1830s. This central time frame of the novel,
the late 1860s, saw many of the trends of the preceding decades in
Spain intensify. Spain witnessed a series of rebellions, the overthrow
of the monarchy, a six-year period of democratic advance followed
by an attempt to restore the previous *status quo*. This became the
Restoration Monarchy and closed off the hope for further social progress. The first thing to note about *The Madness* is that it is set during
a period of tumult, not stability. There are general strikes, military
intervention, repression, political assassination and optimism at the
prospect of meaningful change, followed by disappointment as the
old order re-asserted itself. Such a concatenation of events would
leave a lasting psychological impact on many. In the first chapter we
are introduced to the prevailing forces of law and order: the Catalan
Mossos and the Spanish Guardia Civil, both seen as embodying

repressive practices, autocracy and pro-monarchy reaction. Oller himself had felt optimism during this time of the late 1860s but became disenchanted and conservative by the time of his writing of the book. Though *The Madness* is not to be seen as autobiographical, the author's choice of time frame when he himself was young and optimistic, provides an element of personal journey between the thirty years of the main events and the writing of the novel.

Oller adopted and adapted the realist novel as a way to map social life. Oller uses psychological insight to observe Daniel's breakdown as well as the features of his other characters, all of whom are affluent members of the Catalan middle classes of the time. *The Madness* can be interpreted as part critique of Catalan society of the late nineteenth century and part critique of Spanish political structure. Catalan society of the period was fractured between urban currents in favour of democratisation with a countryside and peasantry heavily supporting the Catholic reactionary movement known as Carlism. We thus find one framing of the novel as Barcelona representing modernity, science, democratisation and progress while the country mostly embodies Catholicism, political reaction and tradition. Struggle was social, cultural, economic, political and religious. Spanish political development broadly followed that of its neighbours France and Portugal where disputes between Catholicism and political liberalism were central. Tensions between tradition and trends of modernisation were as prevalent in Spain as elsewhere. From the 1820s, Spanish political life was marked by conflict between absolutism (reaction) and liberalising currents (reform). Absolutism usually embodied traditional loyalty to the monarchy, the Catholic Church and the preservation of local rights and privileges dating back to the middle ages known as *furs/ fueros*. To the modern reader some of the political movements of the period are archaic and distant, particularly that of the Carlists.

Carlism embodied devotion to God and to their candidate to the Spanish throne. It contributed to two civil wars in Spain, the first between 1833 and 1840 (referred to in the novel as the Seven Years' War). Carlism remained a powerful force in parts of Spain including Catalonia through to the Second Carlist War (1872–76). In *The Madness* there are other references at times to Carlists, such as patrols and so forth, and instances of continuing violence, likely occurring between Carlists and the authorities at various points. Spanish liberals and Carlists had fought one of the most brutal civil wars of the period, causing between 150,000 and 200,000 deaths. The war emerged out of a succession crisis when Ferdinand VII died in 1833, with liberals taking the side of the infant Isabel II and absolutists defending the cause of Ferdinand's brother, Carlos (hence Carlista, follower of Carlos). The Catholic Church is indirectly present as embodying resistance to liberalism, many of whose officials either joined or sympathised with a Carlist movement. The Church is portrayed unsympathetically in the novel. Traditionalists personify Old Spain. Together with their Catholic faith, they embody devotion to an absolutist form of monarchy and fidelity to a strict social hierarchy. The bulk of the Catholic hierarchy, from the Vatican to the dioceses and churches throughout Europe, embraced a frontal opposition to liberalism, embodied by the Syllabus of Errors issued by the Papacy in 1864. Spain is divided, as is the family of Daniel. This division is found expressed in Daniel's parents, his father a freethinker and mother ultimately turning to Catholic mysticism. At the same time, Daniel almost displays a feverish sense of religiosity in his devotion to the political cause he believes in. Daniel passionately believes in his secular religion.

We should avoid being overly influenced by our contemporary

prism when considering Catalonia in reading this innovative Catalan novel. There was little that we could term political currents of nationalism in this period (though there was by the time the book was written) and Catalonia was a full participant in the political life of Spain. Catalonia contributed to the political culture of Spain in terms of new ideas. Barcelona had a vibrant and diverse activity in terms of political publications and pamphlets. The Catalan language remained the vernacular for the majority of the (still mostly rural) population. Cultural revival of Catalan traditions had been growing for decades. Catalonia was at the forefront of an economic upsurge, producing new forms of wealth. Transportation accelerated as the railway began to link populations. Catalonia was rather economically advanced, but tacked onto a state that lagged behind in the development of European capitalism and industrialisation. Catalonia would be much more inclined to adopt the latest cultural and political trends from Europe than was the case in the rest of the Iberian peninsula. This can be seen in the intellectual discussion between the doctor and lawyer at intervals throughout the novel. Catalonia should be seen as a society that is highly receptive to new trends including those around psychology and mental illness, the transmission belt often being France with which Catalonia shares a border. The translation scene was growing in importance, providing ever greater access to new trends in European thought. The linguistic closeness of the Catalan language to French facilitated this process.

The unnamed narrator is a lawyer and much of the discussion in the book takes place between him and his two friends, Giberga, a physician, and the lawyer Armengol. The latter later on also qualifies as a physician. Lawyers played a disproportionate role in political life in Catalonia and the rest of Spain, a tradition that continues today. The Catalan legal system sought to preserve its separation from Spanish authority. Oller read Law at the University of Barcelona and was a qualified attorney. Lawyers and doctors are the archetypal beneficiaries of the rapidly industrialising and transforming society of the mid to late nineteenth century. These professionals represent values of modernity, progress and science. Lawyers offer arguably reasoned interpretation whilst also prioritising order over anarchy Lawyers and doctors are the embodiment of bourgeois progress who receive their training in the university. The law and medicine are terrains of specialist knowledge and we see this expressed in the search for explanation as to the cause of Daniel's madness. Here we also see played out the themes of reason and positivism. Armengol is the principle articulator of the view of scientific discourse as a superior mode of interpretation. Whilst the law offers an opportunity to achieve order, in a similar way medical science can provide order in the realm of the mind. During the mid to late nineteenth century, we see an acceleration in the view that science leads to progress and can explain all phenomena.

The first phase in the novel is set in a period of relative optimism. The reactionary monarchy of Queen Isabel is overthrown in the Glorious Revolution of 1868 and the military hero General Prim offers the possibility of a gradual building of a democratic settlement. The new Spanish Constitution of 1869 was particularly advanced for the period and Prim was its principal architect. Prim was one of the most popular generals of the nineteenth century. Support was widespread amongst progressive and bourgeois currents in Catalonia and other areas of Spain. Hostility to Prim came from ultra-reactionary Catholics, traditionalists and also from radical democratic currents on the left. This period of the late 1860s had been important in the development of Narcís Oller himself. By the time of the novel's publication in 1899, Spain had ceased any programme of meaningful political reform. In wake of the Glorious Revolution, Daniel is elected as a parliamentarian in Madrid though he contributes little beyond an intense loyalty to Prim. Spanish liberals were elitist movements and were not seeking mass democracy. The elite was diverse, being made up of nobles, landowners, merchants, military officers, industrialists and the liberal professions. The liberal elite were divided into conservative (Moderates) and progressive (Progressives) parties that disagreed as to how far reform should be allowed to go. Both traditions used the press to lay out their programmes and communicate with their supporters. Hence the importance for Daniel when he is imprisoned in ensuring his political writings reach a like-minded newspaper readership. Though the narrator and Armengol ridicule Daniel's suspicions around censorship when he was in prison, the last phase before the revolution of 1868 saw a tightly controlled press. It seems more and more that the two friends are complacently satisfied with their own privilege and untroubled by the wider problems of society.

After the end of the Carlist wars in 1839, the military became increasingly important to Spain's politics. However, we should note that army involvement in politics in the nineteenth century could be for progressive purposes. The generals became known as the "swords" of the two main political groups. The *pronunciamiento* became their expression. This was a public declaration by a general and his supporters to change the then government of Spain. However, the *pronunciamientos* did not mean the installation of a military dictatorship but were rather an attempt to remove unpopular governments or tilt them in a new direction. Military leaders were more like instruments of the liberal parties. Progressive generals such as Joan Prim (Joan Prim i Prats – born in 1814 in Reus, Baix Camp) (idolised by Daniel) were widely supported. General Prim was something of a cult figure amongst certain social sectors in Catalonia and was adored by many of the young. The assassination of Prim in 1870 had something of the tone of a national trauma.

When the narrator and his hunting partner visit Daniel's home and mock his collection of Prim paraphernalia, we should remind ourselves that this form of personality cult was quite widespread at the time. Prim was one of the most popular Spanish generals of the nineteenth century and represented the Great Man theory of politics and history. As well as Napoleon, we find the cults of Bolívar in South America and Garibaldi in much of Europe. Portraits and stamps of military heroes were common in this period. Odes and sonnets were also dedicated to these figures so we should not see Daniel's devotion to Prim as necessarily out of the ordinary. Devotion was widespread but what was different about Daniel and Prim was the scale and intensity of his commitment. Daniel does not have one portrait of Prim on his wall but a whole panoply of memorabilia. This idolatry towards Prim should be situated in a current in this period where political ideology sought its expression through attachment to a general. In 1856, for example, the workers of Barcelona launched a general strike with cries of 'Long Live Espartero!' General Espartero was another of these high-profile military figures that progressives and radicals believed could provide political deliverance. Like his predecessor Espartero, we can attribute charismatic leadership to General Prim.

The new Progressive regime led by Prim had overthrown the monarchy of Queen Isabel in 1868 but sought to install a new monarchy. Thus began a search for a candidate in Europe. In 1870 the choice of a German prince for the throne of Spain provoked the Franco-German war of the same year, which ultimately resulted in the Paris Commune. Finally, an Italian candidate was chosen. This was a triumph for Prim but the next day he was assassinated. This assassination of Daniel's hero can be seen as the beginning of a spiral of personal disturbance. We see in Daniel deep attachments to a charismatic individual representing an intense belief system. It remains unknown to this day who assassinated Prim and Daniel believes it to have been organised by a conspiracy involving the Church in Rome, the Jesuits (the bête noire of nineteenth century freethinkers) as well as those opposed to the plan to place an Italian on the Spanish throne. This obsessive paranoia around the assassins and his determination to find the culprits is described as one further manifestation of Daniel's deteriorating mental health. Daniel seems to be as much of a laughingstock amongst the authorities in Madrid as he is amongst his friends in Barcelona. Daniel is what we call a true believer. For this type of individual nothing will dent their belief in the rightness of their cause. This hero worship blinds Daniel, as Prim in office delivered much less democratic reform than was promised. It is significant that Daniel gradually abandons political commitment after the death of his hero.

The family has often been seen as a site of madness. For bourgeois society of the mid to late nineteenth century, the family was required to embody the fundamental values of the new society. This would be the case in society in Barcelona as well as in a small town like Vilaniu. Social stigma was the mechanism used to enforce conformity. It is notable that Daniel's sisters embark on a strategy of character assassination of Daniel amongst his neighbours in Vilaniu. The great fear of all bourgeois, the prospect of a decline in social status, seems to be what determines that the sisters will do all in their power to prevent Daniel marrying a social inferior. Marital alliances were often pivotal in the building of larger economic for-

tunes. The honour of the family is considered particularly important in a small town, where neighbourly gossip has more power to
enhance or destroy reputations. As with the divisive politics in Spain,
the split in Daniel's family is manifested in the town of Vilaniu where
partisans of Daniel or his sisters' point of view appear. The sisters' fear
that they might be excluded from the family inheritance testifies to
the importance of the question of succession in this culture. Daniel
breaks this taboo by choosing as his bride a woman from a rustic
background who seems to lack the gravitas necessary to maintain
the family name. After resisting the sisters' attempts at preventing
his marriage, the arrival of a son for Daniel and his wife means that
the sisters could be completely excluded from the family inheritance.
While visiting Barcelona, Daniel pays a visit to the narrator and
practising lawyer and, in light of the terrible accusations aimed at
Daniel, the narrator, in his capacity as lawyer and friend, suggests
that he resign the claim and come back to Barcelona with his wife
and son. Daniel's stubborn refusal seems to only contribute further
to his condition. After his death, the sisters continue to fight Daniel's
widow by resorting to the favourite strategy of the village: character
assassination. They blame Daniel's wife for an apparent conspiracy to
defraud the family of its wealth. There is little psychological complexity
in the portrayal of women in the novel. They tend to be docile or, as
in the case of Daniel's sisters, hysterical and unhinged.

Following Daniel's withdrawal from politics, he seems to find a
new obsession in the stock market and money making. In the late
1870s Catalonia experienced an intense speculative boom known as
the Gold Fever which gave an impetus to banking and other sectors,
including the railways. Daniel launches himself into this phase with
the intensity he had once devoted to politics. Prior to his obsessive
behaviour in the stock market, Daniel was a gambler. The clinical

term for inflated confidence is grandiosity, and we see several instances of this in Daniel. Collective madness has long been a feature of speculative bubbles, a fervour that Daniel embraces after his political commitment fades. Here Oller is expressing a common critique of Catalan elites and their avid pursuit of money. This speculative fervour produced a new money elite in Barcelona able to engage in conspicuous consumption and Oller was a critic of the vulgarity of the new rich in Catalonia. Members of this new class ranged from solid Catalan manufacturers demanding protective tariffs to safeguard their gains to daring speculators. At the time of the novel's publication in 1899, the Catalan bourgeoisie was the largest in Spain. In 1882 the speculative boom ended, producing an economic crash and downturn which lasted for most of the following decade.

What are the causes of Daniel's madness? Daniel seems to exhibit a number of traits that contribute to his demise. He is politically partisan, stubborn, inflexible, and always unwilling to compromise. The causes of the decline of his mental health range from family, to the political and the financial. As the novel proceeds, Daniel shifts from political idealism to the pursuit of wealth. The explanation most often given in the book is that Daniel comes from a mad family and thus the causation is mostly biological. This hereditary explanation was the main current in scientific understanding of madness at the time. Daniel is prone to bouts of anger, particularly when called upon to be reasonable or to compromise. His obsessions and compulsions, gambling and politics followed by the stock market, are seen as drivers towards his downfall. Oller uses Daniel and his strange behaviors to show us the contradictory motivations, inner turmoil and the highly emotional impulses that some individuals are prone to.

New attempts at the understanding of madness were occurring in Europe and elsewhere in this period. It is Doctor Giberga who provides a medical explanation of Daniel's madness. The narrator's friends and companions Armengol and Giberga are not necessarily sympathetic characters. Armengol is frivolous whilst Giberga provides diagnosis of Daniel's illness with little real human empathy. Giberga also describes Daniel's father's suicide as being simply explained by his being mad and almost having a degree of inevitability about it. This explanation is also seen as sufficient to provide the medical explanation for madness in Daniel, through biology. As with Daniel, his father Ignasi gambled and believed that family members betrayed him. Daniel's battles with his sisters are seen as one more instance of Daniel contributing to his own decline. Yet Daniel's anger at his siblings should be situated within the story that the sisters had contributed to the father's downfall. Whilst Ignasi's poor and indifferent parenting is not considered as an explanatory factor for Daniel, it is provided as part explanation for the behaviour of his sisters. What we might today term a support network for someone undergoing intense psychological pain is absent in the book. Daniel's friends mock him from afar and tend not to take him seriously when they are with him. Oller himself in his memoire spoke of his own experience of depression and periods when he veered from enthusiasm to detachment. There is a sense at the end of the novel that the narrator feels some guilt for his and his friends' failure to be supportive. Whether as a cause or a consequence of his mental instability, the final blow to Daniel is the breakdown of his marriage. Lear-like, bedraggled and unkempt, he rages in his final period at all and sundry, before his committal to an asylum.

Andrew Dowling

THE MADNESS

ONE

He was already the talk of the town when I first met him.

I remember it well. We were halfway through the course of '67 and he was studying to be an agricultural auditor to better manage his properties. I was studying civil law. Armengol, back then my closest friend, came as he did every evening to my lodgings to take a stroll after supper. There had been shots fired on the Rambla the night before and, such was the atmosphere in those days, there were likely to be more that night.

'You know where we could go this evening?' said Armengol as we walked down the street. 'The Cafè de les Delícies. Daniel Serra-llonga is there, and I know you want to meet him. If you want, I'll introduce you both. All I ask is that should he say anything stupid, try not to laugh and leave him to me. He never gets angry with me. I charm him, as they say these days, and he doesn't even realise it.'

'Well, then, it's decided,' I said, happier even than if I had been invited to go to the Romea Theatre where, back then, the great Fontova would make me laugh so much that tears would roll down my face.

Off we went, not stopping until we got to the rotunda at the back of the café, then one of Barcelona's finest. We paused to survey the scene from behind the partition screen in the entrance hall, but Serrallonga was nowhere to be seen.

'Damn him!' Armengol hissed. 'He's probably off gambling.'

'What? He gambles too?' I said.

'Ha! Like a villain. He loves it.'

'Look, look carefully,' I pleaded, desperate not to miss out on the entertainment I had been promised that evening.

We scoured the hallway in front of the columns that held up the mezzanine floor and systematically scrutinised every last person sitting at the tables there, arguing amongst themselves or reading the newspaper. It was just beginning to dawn on me that there was an abundance of men and a strange lack of women there that evening when Armengol let out a five-second-long, 'Well.' I looked over and saw that it was directed towards a fellow just off to the side who, sitting under the magnificent cut-crystal chandelier hanging in the middle of the room, had his head buried in a newspaper that he held out vertically just in front of his nose. The only thing I could make of him were his hands. Armengol went over to him and, greeting him in the most alarming way possible, gave the newspaper a sharp whack in front of his face. The poor recipient jumped out of his skin as if bitten by a snake. Those long, knotted hands I had been looking at quickly went rigid. The left one gripped the newspaper to one side while the other grabbed, mace-like, the closest glass bottle to hand. With the same movement the tall man reared up in a rage, his eyes popping out of his head and his glasses crooked on his nose, looking around for the insolent culprit.

What a devil! I thought as I rushed over to try to stop any trouble. How could he do such a thing? But before I had gone five paces, I saw the danger ebb away. Armengol, with but a flash of his ever-friendly smile, had already excused himself. And Serrallonga, clearly disarmed by what he realised was nothing more than a friendly joke, calmed down, dropped the bottle and was happy to deal with the situation by threatening his friend with a slap across the face.

'I'll clobber you right this moment, simpleton!' laughed Serrallonga. 'I wasn't expecting you. I thought it was some rude reactionary, perhaps some neo who was mortified to see me reading the *Gil Blas*.'

Armengol then introduced me and he and I sat down on either side of Serrallonga, clicking our fingers to get the waiter to serve us a coffee and a glass of something stronger.

Daniel Serrallonga was older than us and must have then been around twenty-five years old. But his pale, hollow face, thick, unruly beard and short, auburn hair made him look a lot older. His eyes, round and grey and hardly visible through the thick glass of his gold-rimmed pince-nez, ever balanced on the bridge of his hooked, flared and twisted nose, added years to him or, at least, provided him with an air of being of a somewhat undefinable age due to his clear lack of youth and the veil of sadness that they conferred on him. He had a big crown with a large, protruding forehead and bushy eyebrows. When listening or thinking his eyes would roll back into his head, hiding his pupils so that only the whites were showing, and the vein on his forehead and wrinkle between his eyebrows would swell and light up as if suddenly congested. He was a lanky man who dressed shabbily and was conspicuous for his terrible taste in ties, all of which were bright in colour and poorly knotted. Generally hot-blooded, he wore his hat pushed back on his head, wide open collars, and never wore gloves or any kind of coat, regardless of how cold it was. But in a surprising contradiction that was the result of ever feeling the need to harmonise his continuous internal agitation with the untiring movement of his limbs, his trousers were always tight and his jacket buttoned-up to the collar so as carry handkerchiefs, books and newspapers in his pockets. He carried an iron-handled cane wherever he went and was never seen without a yellow-stained pipe sticking out of his mouth. If you ever saw him walking in the street, he was often alone with a worried look on his face and would be in such a rush that sweat would drip profusely from his forehead, neck and wrists. He was, in fact, the very person whose strange behaviour I had been told about from time to time by Armengol over the years.

'What, are we all stone broke? Have you lost all your money? Is that why you're here?' said Armengol, pinching Serrallonga's arm. Serrallonga flinched and his glasses wobbled.

'Just you see what happens if you break them!' exclaimed Serrallonga, setting the spectacles more firmly on his nose.

'What ever do you mean?' asked Armengol, insolently.

'I mean, I'll make you pay for them.'

'What cheek! Would you really? What a *fantastic* friend you are!' Serrallonga paused for a moment before smiling and quickly taking off his glasses, which he then handed over to my friend in a gesture of false dignity.

'Here, have them, you fool! If you insist on taking me so seriously, then smash them yourself.'

Seeing that Armengol, in response, was going to put the glasses carefully back in their rightful place, Serrallonga grabbed them off him and, greatly exaggerating their deteriorating friendship, started to insist that he break them.

My eyes grew wide and I bit my lip, but I couldn't stop myself from laughing out loud. Armengol, pretending to take the glasses and smash them on the floor, finally stood up and surprised Serrallonga with a hug before placing the glasses firmly on their owner's nose.

'So, tell me,' he repeated. 'Are you broke or what?'

Poor Daniel turned an embarrassed shade of red at the thought of having to talk about his vices in front of me. As if looking for some way to avoid the question, he bowed his head and stayed silent as he emptied his pipe onto the copy of *Gil Blas* that he had left on the table.

'Come on old chap! This fellow's one of us,' said Armengol, trying to defuse the awkwardness. 'You can tell us. Do you think he's going to go off to your village and tell everyone? You'd know if he was from Vilaniu or not! And you'd better believe that you're the first person from Vilaniu he's ever met. Isn't that right?'

'Well,' said Serrallonga, uncomfortably. 'Why do you want to know if I have money or not? What should I want from you? What do you want from me?'

'No, it's rather what I could offer you,' said Armengol.

'Well thank you. But save your money for a rainy day.'

And as if expecting some kind of applause, he turned to face me and burst out laughing. The teaspoon that, at that moment, I had wedged between my lips meant I wasn't able to humour him and, as I slyly observed him from over the metal handle, I saw in his grinning face that vague sadness that so often betrays the vanity of someone who, in trying to be funny and quick-witted, knows they have failed.

Serrallonga, according to Armengol, was quite the lunatic, shy and prone to the most inexplicable inconsistencies of character. Over the course of the last three years, Armengol had seen Serrallonga go from being a devoted intolerant to a furious rationalist; from an insatiable libertine to holier than a saint; from a hardworking, distrustful miser to the archetypal gambler; from a bookish, first class student to someone who had not read a single book or stepped foot in any classroom throughout the whole course. You wouldn't know him from one day to the next and because of all this his fellow students had given him the nickname *Bandereta*.

But it was when talking about politics that Serrallonga really got going. Back then, the disturbances that were to consume Spain the coming year were getting worse and the fights between the liberals and the conservatives had taken on a worrying animosity. The conservatives, supported by the military led by General Narváez, and the clericalism introduced into the Royal Palace in Madrid by Father Claret and Sister Patrocini, had taken on a certain dictatorial edge as they persecuted, imprisoned and summarily banished anyone and everyone who represented any kind of force or direction within the three Spanish liberal parties. The oppression fomented hatred and ignited a spirit of revolution in the supporters of those being persecuted. Instead of dissipating, the storm clouds grew larger and ever more charged until General Prim, back then the idol of the Catalan youth, found himself having to flee the country. This was despite his being a hero from the African War and a diplomat of such high standing that, in accordance with the wishes of the government and against his own council, he had led the Spanish expedition into Mexico.

Serrallonga, politically indifferent up to then, was so incensed by the scandal that he became a firm supporter of the revolution.

'I read newspapers and more newspapers and get angry: that's all I do these days!'

'Don't get so worked up, old chap,' said Armengol in his own shrewd way, while at the same time flashing me a glance that said: Here we go, he's hooked. Listen up.

'Ye Gods! Do you think I have no blood in my veins? Have you not heard about the shots fired on the Rambla yesterday? Was this why the Mossos de l'Esquadra was created? To shoot at people in the streets? What sly dogs! Honest to God, they don't consider us human beings! I mean, are we going to let them treat us like pariahs, like slaves? Can't you see that this can't be tolerated? What a child you are!'

'So, what do you suggest? As if we could do anything ourselves!'

Serrallonga stopped talking and stared at Armengol, his eyes yellow with concentrated rage and a look of disdain on his lips.

'You'll see what we'll do when we're united,' he said in a low, trembling voice.

Armengol and I struggled to keep our faces straight. What with both of us being quite indifferent to the whole thing, the entire conspiracy seemed rather pointless.

'Oh! Don't laugh, no, at this whole palace business. We'll end up having to beat her out of there with broomsticks and, if not ... then we'll man the cannons!'

'It's all the clergy's fault,' I said in parody of a phrase that until then had been fashionable with the lower-class revolutionaries.

'And still they argue!' cried Serrallonga as he stared at me in such a threatening way that it almost scared me. 'The clergy seems to want round two of what happened in '35. They most likely don't remember what happened to the priests. If you keep squeezing, squeezing ... once the majority have taken up arms, then we'll see. Prim conspires. You'll see what happens when the people are armed! A line needs to be drawn in the sand! A line! The coup is coming!'

Despite coming from Vilaniu, well-known as a town of shouters, Serrallonga usually spoke in a low voice. But in this particular case he found himself raising his voice higher and higher until he reached a point that, in light of the times, started to get rather imprudent, especially considering what he was talking about and the fact that we were surrounded by people we didn't know. In view of this,

Armengol and I started to regret having teased him into his tirade. We glanced around at the faces of the people who, in the middle of the hustle and bustle of the conversations around the room, were closest to us and therefore best able to pick up what our friend was saying. It was then I noticed that the noise in the room was growing in a strange crescendo until suddenly all eyes converged on the entrance and the room fell silent. We looked over and saw the Commander of the Mossos, a tall, large, well-built man with an air of such calmness about him that he looked like someone who had just come to drink a coffee in his favourite bar. He appeared at the entrance dressed, as ever, in an austere turquoise-blue uniform with silver buttons. Walking immediately over to the table in the middle of room, he hadn't yet taken his chair when everybody at the table, without hesitation and as if obeying some mysterious order, suddenly stood up in unison. He stopped where he was and cast an accusing eye around the room in surprise, soon seeing that wherever his gaze fell, the people who met it stood up. Bemused he sat down in defiance of his audience.

'Ah! Not you,' simmered the crowd in silence. 'We won't drink coffee with you, or even in the same room as you, murderer of the people!'

And again, that mysterious common impulse drove everybody away from the tables and upstairs into the round gallery. The ground floor was left deserted except for the Commander and the waiter who, with clenched teeth, quickly served him his coffee. Once alone, the Commander placed his spoon in his cup and, calmly stirring, looked up with disdainful eyes and a disgusting smile on his face to the crowd of people who were now looking down on him. An almighty cry went up.

'*Viva la llibertat!*'

'Death to the murderer!'

'You're not welcome here, bully!'

'Snake!'

'Brute!'

'Traitor!'

'Go to hell!'

Women at the back of the group fainted or ran out screaming while the men, fired up by the tremendous outburst, shouted and cheered and brandished their canes. They continued to threaten the Commander, shaking their clenched fists at him until, having calmly finished his coffee, he got up and shouted towards the crowd:

'Cowards! If any of you want a piece of me, then come on down!'

'I'll have a piece of you!' shouted Serrallonga in a hoarse voice. 'I'll eat your damn liver!'

But just as he tried to barge and elbow his way through the crowd, a worrying looking whirlpool of people started to make its way towards us, gaining in strength. The decorative handrail started shaking dangerously, the women's screams got louder, the sound of firearms filled the air and four pairs of vigorous Guàrdia Civil hands pushed through the crowd of people.

Intent on grabbing our friend, they moved towards us in the midst of a maelstrom of shouts, whistles and threats, mixed in with the jeers aimed at the Mossos Commander as he walked triumphantly out of the ground floor hall, parting the crowd that had barred the entrance.

'Cowards!' shouted Serrallonga, still with the Commander in view and furiously pushing away a truncheon. 'Grab him! Kill him!'

'Kill him! Kill him!' came the useless cry echoing from various other voices.

'Hey! Enough! Enough now!' shouted a towering Guàrdia Civil

sergeant next to me as he stretched out his arm towards our friend and practically dislocated my ribs with the weight of his body.

'Get out, man! Get out while you still can!' came the shouts from all around.

'No! Why should I?' shouted Serrallonga, realising that the raised hands and voices were meant for him. 'Why? Because of the Guàrdia Civil? If they want to arrest me, then they can arrest me! Here I am!'

'No, no, no!' responded the crowd.

'Yes! I'm telling you! Yes! Or are we all chicken?' yelled Serrallonga, bravely sticking out his chest and pushing himself towards the sergeant. 'Sergeant, I'm here, arrest me!'

They arrested him there and then, and that's how Serrallonga found himself imprisoned in the old tower of the Ciutadella. But so preoccupied was he by his rôle as martyr that he wasn't able to comprehend the quite natural distress that led his father, Ignasi, to leave Vilaniu as fast as he could and head off to Madrid in the hope of pulling the few strings he still had in order to get his poor boy out of jail.

We visited him almost every afternoon. He was radiant, brimming with joy at his good fortune and more than happy to tell us, along with an air of commiseration, all about the joys of captivity for those who hate tyranny as much as he did. There within that damp, moss-covered dungeon, lit only by a few rays of light that squeezed in through a slit of only five hand widths high up in the ceiling, Serrallonga would strain his eyes in the semi-dark and write down in pencil manifestos, verses and revolutionary articles on pieces of paper that we would pass him when the guards were distracted. The next day he would pass the papers back to us through the bars so that we could publish them. Armengol and I would take great amusement from reading his puerile exaggerations and not for one moment did it cross our minds to take these snippets and formally present them to a newspaper. So as not to deprive him of the joy that these pieces of paper gave him, however, we told him that they were all being published under varying degrees of cover, and that they were gaining a great deal of attention. At first, the news simply made him happy; later it led him to greater delusions of grandeur.

'What a pity,' he said one day. 'That such caution is required of us (even though it wasn't at all necessary). Because of the jailer's vigilance these papers must be published without my signature! What greater prestige they would have if only the people knew that they came from this prisoner! The man who got revenge for the victims of the Mossos de l'Esquadra!'

He seemed to me to be genuinely shocked. His face, pressed up and quartered against the prison bars, seemed so swollen and sad that I was rather disgusted by the sight of him. Though this feeling was most probably caused by my pained reaction to his inconceivable pretensions.

'Well,' said Armengol, never willing to let up, 'you could always sign them under a pseudonym. And then on your day of triumph you could cast it off as if it were a mask. That way it would be the same as if you had signed your own name from the very beginning.'

Serrallonga, drawing on all of the ideas that he had picked up from the magazines he read at that time, replied to Armengol in a bombastic tone.

'Oh, come on! That would be like belittling a saint at the altar. Popular fanaticism is always moved more by personalities than by arguments, something that people will never understand. The anonymous hero has never awoken any idolatry, without idolatry there are no fanatics, and without fanatics there are no revolutions. Reasons,

reasons… for the people! Someone, I can't remember who, once said: "Reason is a two-handled saucepan that each person picks up as they see fit". The people look for which handle their idols have grabbed, they obsess after that one and care not for anything else. I'm telling you, if my publications so far have made ten converts, they would have made ten million if the people knew from whom and where they came.'

Armengol urged him to speak in hushed tones for a while longer, ridiculing the jailer who was supposedly listening closely to us but who was really keeping as far away from the prisoner as he could.

'Always… scoundrels! Always!' exclaimed the poor prisoner.

We went back to what we were talking about before and agreed that all of our revolutionary's political venting would from then on be published under the rather brilliant pseudonym *El Barricadero*, a name of Armengol's creation.

As we were leaving, I admitted to being quite scandalised by Serrallonga's high opinion of himself and how he was elevating his childish prank from Café de les Delícies to heroics. Armengol laughed.

'He's a visionary, man! He's a special case! And he'll always see himself like that. Look at how easily he thinks that we'll publish his nonsense!'

'And don't you think it's rather terrible of us to let him believe we would? What if tomorrow he's released, and he sees we've been lying?'

'Oh, come on, man! Meanwhile he's happy and we keep him busy. This is why I'm doing it in the first place. Perhaps this time in prison and the disappointment that it brings will cure him of his innate silliness.'

'He thinks he's some kind of celebrated avenger and focus of popular idolatry! Oh, of course, of course!'

And so, instead of sharing a deep sense of compassion with our imprisoned comrade as we should have done, we went home laughing like the two boys we were. Things carried on in this way until early one afternoon Armengol appeared on my doorstep with a larger than normal smile on his face.

'You will never guess who came to visit me just three hours ago!' he exclaimed. 'The *Bandereta*, *El Barricadero*, our very own Daniel Serrallonga!'

'What do you mean?' I replied sleepily, watching the hailstorm clouds that had been gathering in the sky above us for the last few hours.

Armengol collapsed into my rocking chair and, rolling the cane he had on his lap between his palms, told me in fits of laughter about the meeting he and Serrallonga had just had. Apparently, Serrallonga had come running up the stairs unaware of the natural stiffness that legs suffer from after two months under lock and key and had reached Armengol's flat on the fourth floor in a terrible state of near exhaustion. Armengol, seeing his friend in that way and taking it for emotion, got emotional himself and, with tears in his eyes, reached out his arms and embraced him. Serrallonga, however, pushed him away and sat down to catch his breath. He wiped the sweat off his brow, neck and wrists and, once he had cooled down, asked with anxious, impatient eyes for the scraps of paper with his writings and the newspapers in which they had been published. Ever untroubled by these sorts of things, Armengol had been putting off inventing an excuse until the announcement of Serrallonga's release and so was rather stuck for words. He chewed it over briefly, biting down hard on his bottom lip and all the while staring at the new cane that the ex-prisoner had bought and was now shoving up against his ribs.

Serrallonga started to lose his patience at the dithering and demanded again to see the beloved papers he had been dreaming about and which he had come to collect.

'So, where are they? Didn't you tell me you were saving them? Come on, get them out.'

'Yes, but… yes, but…,' stammered Armengol.

'But what?' replied Serrallonga, tersely.

'But should you really be taking them, considering the atmosphere these days?'

'Oh, come on! Don't worry about that, you invertebrate! Look, give them to me. In fifteen minutes I have to be at the inn to meet my father. Listen to this: he says that he has promised the general to keep me at his side at all times and that I have to go back to Vilaniu!'

'Ah!' said Armengol, feeling a little more relaxed. 'I've got it! I've got it! Thank God!' He turned to face Serrallonga. 'I mean, you're going? I'm so sorry to hear that! But I'll be sure to send them to you.'

'What?' said Serrallonga. 'Why? Give them to me now, man! This is why I've come. I'll take them myself. They won't find them because they won't search me, I assure you. But at least let me see them. I understand why you wouldn't bring them to the prison, but don't deny me them now. Come on!'

'No, no. I won't deny you them.'

'So?'

'It's just that I don't have them here on me. The truth is that so as to afford them the greatest possible diffusion, I left them with a friend.'

'As God is my witness! And if he loses them?'

'No, old chap! Of course not. Just you relax. I'll be sure to send them to you.'

'It'd be easier to go and get them now. Let's go. I'll accompany you.'

Armengol told me that he had to spend another fifteen minutes inventing excuses and subterfuge so as to worm his way out of the situation and drop poor Daniel off at the inn, instilled with the hope of receiving in Vilaniu something that did not exist.

TWO

Serrallonga was back in his village and completely oblivious to our rather cruel trick, but it didn't sit well with me. What if he realised that his papers weren't going to arrive? And what if he discovered that none of them had ever seen the light of day? Not even in newspapers such as *El Trueno Gordo*, *El Vengador* or even *El Rigoletto*, places where he assumed they would most certainly have been published. Could he not return at some unexpected moment and bash our skulls in with his cane? In his most furious moments, Daniel was capable of this and much more and in this case he had more than a good enough reason to go that far. But Armengol's ingenuity, along with a very sad turn of events, was to free us from that most absolute danger.

So as to escape the pickle he found himself in, it occurred to Armengol, cunning as ever, to go to ground for some ten to twelve days before sending a letter to Serrallonga. This letter expressed his desperate alarm that Serrallonga hadn't yet received the bundle of newspapers that he had sent and conveyed his deepest fear that the package had been imprisoned in the Post Office's black box. He also expressed his regret that he wouldn't be able to get his hands on any further issues of the publications due to the rigorous persecution that the press was then under and the fact that they had sold out within just a few minutes.

'This way,' said Armengol, ever willing to fan the flames of the *Bandereta*'s belief in ominous Government (you will recall the incident that landed him in jail), 'he will most surely believe in the existence of the bundle of newspapers. If the Post Office says that they haven't seen any copies of *Vengador*, *Rigoletto* or *Trueno Gordo*, he would simply take it as part of their conspiracy and the truth would pass him by. He's bought some absolute whoppers in his time: he's a lot more gullible than you might think and, in this case, we have in our favour his passionate blindness to human understanding, flowing ever serenely into his eyes.'

That said, I was not one hundred percent convinced and found it difficult to see the situation in as favourable a light as my friend, who one might say was more happy-go-lucky than ever. For my part, my anxieties increased as I worried that, at any moment, Armengol might turn up at my house with his head split open while far away in Vilaniu, with every post that came and went without receiving any letter, Serrallonga spat more and more hate and bile against the ominous Government. After fifteen days of alarming silence I bumped into my friend in the street. He wore a long face and a veil of sadness covered his eyes.

'What's up with you today?' I asked.

'Here,' replied Armengol, sadly handing me an envelope. 'This will explain everything.'

It was Don Ignasi Serrallonga's obituary.

'Oh my God,' I said, morbidly.

Both Armengol and I took his death to be the natural result of the worry, yearning and exhaustion that the poor man had suffered while his son had been in prison. Being naturally rather timid and sickly, the many arduous journeys to Madrid coupled with the highs and lows and hours of growing weakness that the man no doubt went through to secure the freedom of the apple of his eye might well have been the end of him. The proximity of the event made us even more suspicious. Later that day, we chanced upon someone from Vilaniu, and he told us more about the man's death. Giberga studied Medicine and had been the one to first introduce Armengol to Daniel Serrallonga.

Offering to give us the long version of the story, we sat down at a table at an almost deserted mid-afternoon Suïs Bar and, with a beer for each of us, Giberga started to explain:

'What's more, he didn't die like you might think. Don Ignasi committed suicide.'

'He committed suicide?' we replied, feeling terrible for Daniel's misfortune. At that sweet, sweet age of hopes and illusions, we simply couldn't conceive the absurdity of killing yourself.

'Yes, Don Ignasi was mad'.

'Well, well. Here we go. You and your madness!' I exclaimed impetuously. 'All you medical students suffer from the same problem. For you, everything already has an answer: anyone who is different in a moral sense, isn't all there. For those who listen to you lot, there seems to be no possible diversity outside of the subject. You admit to a variety of hands, arms, legs, etc., but only because the eyes and fingers can't possibly deny them. But anything immaterial, anything elusive and, therefore, intangible won't fit into any of your moulds, and you can't stand it. But why, if there are hunched bodies and wonky eyes, could there not be hunched or wonky souls?'

'Well, let's not argue,' said Pròsper Giberga, one of those jealous pedants of the natural sciences who, thanks to a certain thoughtless despotism, look with Olympic disdain upon any and all objections that come from other fields. 'Let's not argue about these crossed-eyes or hunched backs. We call them *affected* to differentiate them from the others.'

This explanation seemed to me rather scornful and, suspicious of the coolness with which he argued his case, I decided to stay quiet. Even though this meant allowing him *carte blanche* to present us with all his most fervent beliefs. Giberga lit a cigar and, as if oblivious to my reaction, or perhaps simply for his own self-satisfaction, he proceeded to rub further salt in the wound by telling us Don Ignasi's whole sorry story.

'They say that he was once a lieutenant with the Miquelets and that, with the Seven Years' War over, he started to court Engracieta Torner, the only daughter of a rich – and dead – notary public from Vilaniu. He managed to finish his studies and pass the final exam before, in accordance with the young lady's laggard custodian, he married her and bought the notary office recently vacated by her dead father.'

'Well, so far, all I see is a motivated, hardworking man,' I said, trying to give the story a somewhat positive twist.

'And if she loved him…,' added Armengol, already enjoying the somewhat tense situation developing between the two of us.

'That's the thing!' continued Giberga, pretending to misunderstand. 'It seems that they were both rather fooled by each other. The whole situation blinded them (so says my father, a life-long general practitioner) to the extent that they both ended up believing that they were in love with each other. Both of them, thanks to their innate way of being, were a pair of passionate dreamers, as you say yourselves. She was simple and romantic, a lunatic at heart; he was (as we have said) reckless enough to exchange the comforts of a house and home for the adventures of war and possible death. What happened was that after about a year they had fallen out and grown apart. Engracieta, having already given birth to Daniel, started looking for solace elsewhere, finding it in the church. So extreme was her devotion that she ended up as some kind of mystic. The ex-lieutenant, furious at this seemingly hypocritical change of character, started finding distraction in the casino and once again took up his venerable gambling habits. Homelife became hellish and a miserable Engracieta died in childbirth. It was Daniel's second sister, a hunched little thing called Carolina.'

'He has two sisters?'

'This Carolina and the ingenious Adela,' he laughed.

'She's intelligent, then?' I asked.

'Intelligent? She's a devil in a skirt, causing trouble wherever she goes! In only two years, she's courted at least four or five boys in Vilarniu. And as her father used to spend every night at the casino tables, the boys would take advantage of her. Daniel's main problem will be his sisters because the other one, the hunchback, is even worse than her elder sister.'

'Goodness! She doesn't *smoke*, does she?' asked Armengol in jest.

'No, I don't mean that at all. But who cares? She's uglier than a ghoul. I mean, rather, her mouth and what comes out of it!'

'So, crooked in both body and soul: just what you were both discussing before. But the question is: wouldn't an ex-lieutenant with the Miquelets know how to solve the problem?'

'Ignasi wasn't close to his daughters until his sister Igualada died. She was the one who had looked after the girls after the mother died.'

'It doesn't seem as if this sister of his, from what you say, did a particularly good job raising them!'

'No. The poor woman isn't to blame. It was all she could do to take them in. Her brother was convinced that they weren't even his.'

'Oh, fantastic!' chimed in a laughing Armengol, finding this ex-lieutenant notary increasingly entertaining.

'Three or four years after taking them in, the aunt suffered from an ataxia that turned into total paraplegia.'

'In layman's term, man,' I said. 'What do you mean?'

'I mean she was paralysed, stuck in a wheelchair until her death. And the girls grew up untamed, like wild trees.'

'If Adela is tall and well-built, then fine,' said Armengol. 'But from what you say, the hunchback seems more like a trunk with a head.'

'And so, if I understand correctly,' I said, 'the three siblings have never lived together in the same house.'

'More or less. When has Daniel seen them? During the last two years' holidays. He acted the father figure.'

'Well, well, well! What confusion!' cried Armengol.

'This is what I'm telling you. Well, now you'll see. If the father had been a sensible man, would he have left a pair of girls who should have stayed by his side under the tutelage of a sick woman who wasn't able to care for or educate them? If, as has been shown, closeness breeds caring, then what fruit could that separation have produced? According to those in the know, Don Ignasi saw his girls only three times in twenty years. With a separation like that during the period of their lives when the heart is formed and affections between family members are sown, how could they later learn to love their father and Daniel?'

'Yes, but if the man thought they weren't his…'

'He was delirious: no one has ever understood the basis of this suspicion. One that drove a mystic to mania and two girls, especially the hunchback, to being crushed under the weight of their father. A mania of persecutions of the like I am only just getting started with!'

Armengol and I met the medical student's assertions, that every Tom, Dick or Harry was mad, with mocking smirks.

'What I'm saying is that you should add it all up. Firstly: coming from a good family and being halfway through his studies, he leaves it all behind and goes off to risk life and limb for something that has nothing to do with him. That's madness, and don't you deny it.'

'Well I do deny it,' I blurted out, leaving myself open to criticism and accusations of madness from that slip of a wise man. 'I deny it because I believe in ideals and I understand the sacrifice of one's life for those ideals.'

Armengol just laughed.

'Secondly,' continued Giberga with aplomb and increasing seriousness. 'He started his own business, went back to studying something that he didn't like and settled down with a simple girl whose feelings were the polar opposite of his own.'

'She was the heiress!'

'And is it not delirium to sell yourself short when you are strong and agile enough to get ahead? Thirdly: once he saw that it was impossible to command respect from others, he turned to gambling as if it were a remedy. He abandoned his office, got into debt and exasperated his already hard-done-by wife, turning against her and ruining her life all because she, a mother first and foremost, didn't want to accompany or push him down that path to ruin. He suffered terribly and, unable to leave his vices, he didn't know how to return the peace to his wife that he himself had taken from her, while also being unable to leave her and finish the whole business there and then. Instead of this, instead of reducing the turmoil, he continued to live with her and dishonoured her with his false accusations.'

By now, a seriousness had descended on the conversation and

a sudden sense of indignation came over both Armengol and me.

'So say that he was despicable, then!' I shouted.

'No,' said the indominable student, sternly. 'I say that he was ill and irresponsible, just like all madmen. The blurring – as we'll call it – of his perceptions was the cause of the first of his disasters. The effects of these incited him to fury and distorted his reality even more. This explains how he was able to believe that his wife had betrayed him. These kinds of illnesses create vicious circles of cause and effect.'

I should admit that I was unable to shake off a dark foreboding about what Giberga had told us. The subject of the vicious circle aroused in me – I'm not sure why – an image that became coarse and ridiculous when applied to intellectual functions: I thought of a waterwheel returning water to the same well. Giberga had hurt me and I could no longer understand him. It was just the way I was.

'Murder begets murder, does it not?' continued Giberga. 'It's obvious: the abandoned girls were later unable to love or respect their father. Someone had told them that the person who had abandoned them was the same person who had sacrificed their mother and so to them, Don Ignasi was a monster. Shut away from him, their hatred had stewed for so long that there was only one thing for it to do: burst. And burst it did. Not even the sight of him as a wizened, destitute old man – the natural result of a turbulent life and the early onset of old age – was of any effect. Made lustful for revenge for themselves and their mother, so bitterly did they attack him that it enraged him even more. Those accusations eventually sent the poor man completely mad and, when he got to the prison where his son was, the need to make this other kind of effort perhaps momentarily suspended the development of his principal illness in a kind of "lesser of two evils" reflex. But he gets to Vilaniu with

Daniel and what had the daughters done? They had robbed the old man and left. The town was full of people amusing themselves with all manner of dishonourable assumptions regarding those dreadful girls who had already discredited the man greatly in the eyes of the people. The father reached such a state of agitation that he shot himself in the head. And so badly did he do it that he lived on for another eight days.'

'And where are those awful girls now?' I asked.

'As the gambler most likely had very little left at home, their brother convinced them to return while the father was still alive.'

'What insolence!'

'This is why I'm telling you to feel sorry for Daniel. When they turned up, he rejected them. I've heard that it was really quite terrible. But according to the neighbours, after all the shouting they calmed down and the boy, standing before the majesty of the corpse, ended up letting them in. How will it all pan out? We'll see. But for me, Daniel came into this world a marked man.'

'Whatever! Go on, away with you now!' shouted a laughing Armengol. 'What madness! You need to take a long, hard look at yourself!'

THREE

During the following summer holidays, I went with my cousin – a keen hunter – to Bondelit. We spent three days in the mountains there and hunted very little, but tanned our skin brown and started to rebuild the muscles that one loses when in the city. We were high up on the mountain ridge when an unexpected turn gave way to a dazzling, panoramic view of the Flors Valley. In the middle of the valley, dotted with villages, farms and country houses and half hidden by the copses of trees that run along the streams and paths that surround it, we spotted Vilaniu, the administrative centre of the area. Seeing it brought back vivid memories of Serrallonga's story and his household's tragedy of deliriums and passions that seemed impossible against a backdrop of such peacefulness. I thought a lot about Daniel, who I hadn't seen since his time in prison and I was overcome by a strong desire to pay him a visit, to meet up close those dreadful girls, as Giberga had called them, and to compare how I imagined the places with the real, tangible ones where the events had actually taken place. I had told my cousin all about these events when they happened, and we both thought back to them as we contemplated Vilaniu, just below us as the crow flies. As my cousin had also taken an interest in the events, awaking the same feeling within him as it had in me, it didn't take us long to decide to overlook the problems a detour to the town would present us with.

And so we went. On the outskirts of the town we asked a farmer for directions. He was coming back from ploughing his field and was leading his mule by the reins. He had laid the plough across the saddle pack on its back. When we mentioned the name Serrallonga, he replied that Daniel had just recently done the town a great service by setting up an iron foundry there, but that he didn't know if he was in Madrid at that moment "as a Member of Parliament" or not.

'What!?' I blurted out, scarcely believing what I was hearing.

My cousin, glancing over at me, advised prudence. Once in the town and having been told where Daniel's house was, we went straight there. We were eager to see if the owner was there and, of course, we wanted the chance to meet his sisters.

The house in town still carried its traditional name, Torner, and was located on a steep, narrow, dark and winding street called Carrer de l'Església. The house had two floors, an attic and a long, first floor balcony. The façade, some eight metres wide and with 18th-century carvings, was black with grime, lending the whole place a rather unpromising aspect. The most ominous feature, however, was the entrance. The doorway had been given a thin coat of white paint while the pine reception door was unpainted and stained by the passing of the years. Pushed open, it gave way with an almighty metallic creak.

It was getting late in the day. The only light to the stairwell came from a skylight above and it was already quite dark. Despite the gloom and the apparent absence of anyone else, we carried on up the stairs, shouting out greetings as we reached the first floor.

Would you believe it?! The two door panels were wide open to all and sundry, but nobody was at home. If there had been anyone in the house and they hadn't heard the creaking of the hallway door or our repeated calls as we went up the stairs, they must have been completely deaf.

Shouting out again for the umpteenth time, we looked at each other briefly and, wondering in silence at the lack of reply to our shouts, finally dared to enter the room that presented itself to us. There were two doors on the right, one on the left and another set into the wall at the far end. All were open and there was nobody to be seen. It was as if the house had been burgled. The first door on the right opened into a long room that was furnished with chairs and sofas covered with pink cloth. Towards the back of the room were other pieces of furniture bathed in light coming from the side, like the other rooms. The exception to this was the room at the end that opened up onto a balcony leading to some garden or access route. As such, it became clear to us that the building was built at an angle.

We shouted out another greeting at the door to the long room.

Still no one.

We looked through the door on the left. It was the kitchen, full of reflections from the Valencian tiles where the dull light fell that filtered through a discreetly half-opened window. The central door, the one on the opposite side of the room, led into the dining room. It was a small, wallpapered room, adorned with dizzying green and yellow baubles. That was also deserted. Only the second door on the right remained for us to peer inside, and so we did.

'Hello! Is anyone home?'

Nobody answered and so, in we went.

We found ourselves in a study once used by notaries public, but that was now Daniel's. The row of sealed cupboards that covered three of the walls seemed to be speaking to us from the very moment we walked through the doorway. At the end of the room was a brand-new bureau and behind it on the wall were a great many photographs, lithographs and etchings of General Prim.

'Goodness me!' exclaimed my cousin in fits of laughter. 'It's as if he's producing them to order!'

'Shut up,' I whispered, nudging him with my elbow and moving closer to get a better look at them. 'Daniel's madness is getting worse. As a student he never shut up about Prim. He knew everything about him by heart: which day he joined the Cossos Francs; when and why he was made captain, then commander, then lieutenant colonel, then colonel, then brigadier, then general, then deputy, then senator, then Count of Reus, then Viscount of Bruc, then Marquis of Castillejos then Grand Duke of Spain, et cetera, et cetera. It seems clear that Prim has gone from being his idol to being his god.'

There were representations of Prim from throughout his life, from colonel on up: Prim from the Seven Years' War, Prim the defender of Reus, Prim in the African War, Prim in Mexico, Prim from the September Revolution. Now as a half-portrait, then as a full portrait. Here as a patriot, there dressed as a soldier, his chest covered in crosses. Over here, mounted on horseback at Castillejos brandishing the Spanish flag amongst a maelstrom of the dead and dying; further away, his sword aloft as he jumps across a trench at Tetuan. There was an impulsive, fearless Prim on the battleground, a hypnotizing vision as soldier and Catalan voluntary; Prim the legendary living hero, acclaimed by the people under various triumphal arches and covered with flowers. Prim the exalted orator with his speeches to the masses from the terraces of public palaces; Prim the politician advising against the expedition to Mexico from the steps of the senate, his frock coat tightly done up and his large forehead uncovered, all set into a frame of laurel and oak, adorned with heraldic shields won through his prose and patriotic service…

There it was: the most eloquent and palpable expression of how far Daniel Serrallonga's fanaticism had gone towards the last great Spanish captain of our time. Who would have thought that with the fading away of that idiosyncratic Catalan leader, the full weight of Castilian pride would come tumbling down for want of a guide?

In those moments I was reminded of the two stains on the otherwise brilliant biography of Reus' favourite son: the help that, due to personal ambition, he once gave to the moderates who were bombarding the sons of his very own region; and, as a good bourgeois fellow from the provinces, the allowance he would concede to the Castilians, almost certainly adoringly, in regards to the ill-fated synonymy of Spain and Castile. If the second of these two stains found no graphic expression in Daniel's collection, the first one, which he did admit, didn't feature in his engravings either. This was perhaps due to Daniel's selection or to the insurmountable dislike that the act had provoked in the very same artists who painted him.

At any rate, all those portraits had been brought together through the enthusiasm of a young man who had almost certainly never exchanged even a single word with their subject. And we found it strange, quite original, and hilarious in equal measures.

'What a curious chap,' whispered my cousin in my ear.

No sooner had he said this than we heard footsteps behind us. We turned around in surprise and our sharp movement was greeted by a shocked scream.

'Help, help! Thieves!'

Of course, we had forgotten that we had come straight in from the forest. We were carrying rifles and were dressed like a couple of dusty, dirty-faced villains. We ran out of the room to confront the source of the shouting, to silence her calamitous shrieks and to calm her down by showing her who we were, our honourable intentions and how wrong she was to worry. But her screams were so loud that, just as we were reaching the stairs down which she was fleeing in terror, there also arrived from the floor above, flying down the stairs five steps at a time, a young man with blond hair and a tall but chubby woman who was as white as a sheet.

'Help, help,' she repeated in a trembling, terrified voice.

The first woman (an elderly, hunched, plump specimen) and the other two then came together in a huddle and all three, trembling like quicksilver and hanging on to each other for dear life, found themselves grouped together like a bundle of sticks on the landing, scared witless and watching our every move. At the same time, our faces burning with shame, our legs shaking and completely lost for words and thoughts, we tried to think of what to say. The situation, if not dangerous, was both serious and rather unpleasantly brutal for all involved. There was nothing else for it.

'Listen! Listen!' we shouted repeatedly in trembling voices. 'For the love of God!'

This went on for a while until it miraculously occurred to me to garnish my bungling entreaties with names from the Serrallonga family in the hope that we might make a connection with them.

'Adela! Carolina!… We aren't thieves!… Listen!… Please!'

Hearing themselves addressed by these names gave them more confidence. They stopped shouting for help and all three of them started to let out sighs and gasps of relief. It was then clear that we were standing before the ladies of the house.

'Forgive us and please don't be afraid. I am a friend of Daniel's and, hoping to see him as we came down from hunting up at Bondelit, we committed the imprudence of inviting ourselves in without so much as passing by the guesthouse to get changed.'

My tongue had finally begun to untangle itself and the women's hearts calmed down. The three-person bundle came undone and, all the while moaning and sighing in a clearly exaggerated manner, the girls allowed us to approach and take them by the hand so as to help them down from the chairs they were standing on in the entrance hall. The young man who had been following them, still as yellow around the gills as the girls, went off to the dining room from where he appeared after a minute with a bottle of wine and a couple of glasses.

'Here. Drink. This'll cool you down.'

My cousin and I didn't say a word. Not because we were out of breath, but rather because of the awkwardness of so many moans and breathless sighs. Really, truth be told, it was all rather exaggerated, especially the moans coming out of hunchback's mouth. I mean, what had she seen to make her first cry out? A pair of young men, dressed more or less in hunting clothes, who had walked into her brother's office. This was something that happened, frankly, quite often not only in villages, if one wished to take things to the extreme, but between good friends. And, with our rifles slung across our backs in the most honest possible way, like people waiting for the owner of the house to show up – having already announced our arrival – and entertaining ourselves by looking at pictures of General Prim! Were we picking any locks? Had we rummaged through any papers on the table? Were we fingering through the few antique books that sat under the window? No! So why would anyone think we were robbers, fill the house with people, and make such a large mountain out of such a small molehill? What's more, Adela and the blond boy hadn't seen anything and had no idea what was happening. They had heard the frenzied shouts coming from the floor below and, seeing the bulk of two armed men against the light behind Carolina, they had thought the worst. These considerations, flashing through our minds now that the primary shock had passed, started to make us reconsider our apologising to them, something that always seems to happen when one feels a victim of another's exaggerations.

As we were waiting quietly for the best moment to clear everything up while keeping our moral obligations intact, the hunchback took a good gulp of wine and wiped her lips on her shawl.

'These things just won't do!' she exclaimed in a hoarse, insolent voice. 'Who said that you could come into our house like this?… Oh!… Oh!… Oh!… and what a fright you've given me!'

'It's true,' we replied. 'Anyone would assume that we had sneaked in. But it's not like that. As the doors weren't closed, we just assumed that there was somebody at home. The doorbell wasn't working, and we shouted dozens of times on the stairs and throughout the house so that someone might hear us.'

Adela put on her smoothest tone of voice and tried to appear reasonable.

'It's just that we were doing a piano class on the very top floor of the house and Margarida was up there cleaning.'

'I thought I heard the doorbell,' added the boy.

'Ah!' exclaimed the hunchback, still with an aggressive tone. 'Why do you think I went downstairs? I, too, heard the doorbell! But who would expect anyone to dare invite themselves in past the reception?'

'Truly,' said my cousin, who was far better at explaining himself in a calm manner than I was. 'We went too far: forgive us. But please believe us when we say that it was completely by accident. We asked for permission before looking through every door. If we invited ourselves into the office, it was without realising it. We were attracted, like moths to a flame, by your brother's curious collection of portraits. If we had thought that we would frighten anybody, and therefore been on the receiving end of such a bitter reprimand, even having to ask you all for forgiveness, believe us, believe that we would never have crossed that threshold.'

'No, no, no. It's all clear now!' said Adela, clearly upset by Carolina's insolence as she continued to grumble and interrupt us with sardonic, salty assertions and furious sighs.

Adela got up and came over to shake our hands before telling us to save our breath and inviting us into the long room. Trying desperately to excuse ourselves, we begged her to let us leave with news of her brother, Daniel, whom we would have liked to have seen. But such was her insistence and her evident intention to repair the injury inflicted on us by her sister, it would have been churlish not to follow her.

Adela and the young piano teacher took us by the hand as it was too dark to see and led us into the room with the pink covers. She lit a lamp on a round table in the corner with a withered crochet cover and practically forced us to sit on the sofa. Our rifles between our legs, we were flanked by our new acquaintances, who occupied the neighbouring armchairs. The hunchback was nowhere to be seen. A furious creature, she had neglected to join us and had decided to stay outside in a fit of stubbornness.

Adela was distant. She was one of those girls who is attractive from far away thanks to her stature and physical proportion, and a certain sensuality that resided principally in her litheness, in the freshness of her skin and the somewhat questionable way she swung her hips. This, too, made her attractive to look at, and was in perfect harmony with the rosy whiteness of her skin and her pretty, tobacco brown hair, silky smooth and lightly curled. But her small, cat-like, green-grey, gold-flecked eyes and snub nose, doubly diminished in comparison with her rather large mouth that she opened wide and gurned when she spoke or laughed curbed any initial sympathetic impulses from one who might be looking for any signs of intelligence, idealism or sweetness. As did the excessive width of her upper lip that was often inflated at the edges due to her many disdainful snorts and, finally, the rectangular, almost primate-like shape of her jutting lower jaw, solidly set with large, crooked and discoloured teeth. Her bosom was ample, and she held her head high whilst clearly exaggerating her movements and giggles to charm admirers, the men to whom she had appeared so attractive from afar. The same objective was manifest in her way of dressing: exaggerated lines covered in striking and irrationally placed decorations and inharmonious colour combinations. That's the way she was, at least that day, when I found myself staring at her pink cotton skirt, paired with a blood red blouse and a stupendously wide blue belt that she wore like a cummerbund laced together at the front with tassels that ran down almost to her feet. Her blouse was open at the neck, allowing her to air her double chin and whiter than white nape on which gleamed a layer of golden down and a thin cherry-coloured ribbon complete with medallion that she wore as a necklace.

I make no mention of the ornaments that adorned her skirt and the edges of her blouse, or the ribbon, also cherry in colour, that she wore on the middle of her head alongside her abundant braids. Nor will I describe her earrings and the multitude of rings she wore on her fingers, as it should be sufficient to say that in everything, absolutely everything (and even more so if one takes into account the village environment in which the girl found herself), she showed an immoderate wish to stand out from the crowd. I also ignore, if giving in to this desire, which for her must have been irresistible, the fact that she sat down next to me as she did, balanced on one buttock and parting her legs in such a way that one could see the patent leather she wore on both feet and a good part of her undergarment, speaking to me with her arm resting on the chair so that it pushed right up against her breasts.

That said, it would be unfair to her if I did not mention here the friendliness with which she received us. She seemed to be genuinely upset that we had made the journey in vain, telling us how easy it would have been to achieve our objective if only we had undertaken our trip in reverse: Daniel had gone to Madrid just two days before. She told us that he wasn't exactly the MP for Vilaniu, as we thought, but rather the local representative. She told us all about the elections and how hotly disputed they had been. We saw that her brother's victory had left her rather emotional and so we took advantage of the occasion to ask her to repeat a number of things that, under the circumstances, we found side-splittingly hilarious.

'You, sir, know my brother. He's very big-headed, isn't he? Oh! He and I get along very well. Now and again I tell him "What a pity we are siblings!" because I like my men like that, like him, so... so forthright, passionate about everything, refusing to take one step back even if the world itself collapses. I don't know! That's a man for me: they all should be like this... He does everything enthusiastically, everything. You, sirs, have already seen his collection of General Prim portraits. Isn't it strange? He says: "Is this man from Spain?... Well then everyone, everyone must support him. Opinions and ideas? They are all either fantastic or terrible depending on who interprets them: the man does it all".

'Clearly,' I said, encouraging her to entertain us a little more so as to flesh out the explanation I wanted regarding the unexpected reconciliation of the siblings.

'He has a lot of talent, a lot! They'll see, the rôle he'll play in Madrid! They won't be able to shut him up, no. Well! And here,

here… They'll see him coming, alright! Oh! They won't happen, no, the things that went on in the Galcerans' time! Right this moment, he is already better known amongst many people and more talked about than Rodon. You need only to see the look on his wife's face! You'll see: She's a… well, lady, despite her being nosier than whoever… a lady who, poor deceased Lady Isabel… Oh! She plumped herself up like a turkey. She thought she was the queen around here, you know? And now, seeing that there is another family that is not only her equal, but that beats her in all areas… Now, when she saw that Daniel was setting up a great political association and was going to be a Member of Parliament… But, what am I doing telling you all about Vilaniu? You don't have the foggiest! I might as well tell you about the moon. Go ahead, please.'

Well, I thought. You've already said quite enough young lady! Quite enough! You've already given up the secret that I was looking for! What a brother! What you love most is the social importance that he brings to you. And your insignificance here in this unknown rural corner of the world doesn't matter one jot to you because, for you, this is the world. Oh, *vanitas vanitatis*! And aren't you happy about it, you crazy lot!

Then, taking up the conversation once again with all the energy of the dim-witted orator who, coming across new listeners, can repeat again and again the most exhausted parts of their repertoire, she regaled us with her brother's great moral conditions, as put to the test by Carolina.

'Because…' Here she stood up, tiptoed to the door to see who was listening and, turning and lowering her voice, continued. 'Because, to put up with this girl requires the patience of a saint, believe me. Now she's asleep, thank God. I was worried that she had had an accident.'

'She suffers from accidents?'

'Yes, sir. She has epilepsy. Everything comes from that. Indeed, if it weren't for this, I think Daniel would have kicked her out, and I would have been first in line to tell him to do so. Because… well, as you have seen, she has a way of bringing out the worst in people. He can't stand her. She's to blame for everything. For example, she doesn't want to get dressed, she doesn't want to go anywhere. Of course not, she's a hunchback! Despite this, though, a well-turned-out person is always more pleasing to the eye, don't you think? The reputation of our name and our position requires us. But, what's more, one's sister? Would it not be worth a small sacrifice for her to help and protect me? Well, you wouldn't think it. So very stubborn! And her accidents, giving us such shocks that make it impossible for us to contradict her! Here you go: today, for example, I'd like to invite you to stay for dinner, you being Daniel's friends… but I can't… I don't dare. And my brother, how happy he would be!'

And she would have carried on like that for the next four hours had we not, eager to get cleaned up and to rest, made clear our resolve to leave.

'What do you reckon?' I asked my cousin once out in the street.

'That, my friend,' he replied, 'is a madhouse. What madness! What misery!'

FOUR

Four years passed without me hearing anything about Daniel, and had it not been for bumping into Armengol in a bar in Barcelona, it would have been even longer.

'Hello hello!' grinned Armengol. 'What are you doing here? It's great to see you!'

'You too! What a coincidence!'

'I'm just back from Madrid. Oh, and you can take your hat off to me: I am now officially a graduate doctor. I arrived at two this morning because of some Carlists stopping the train at Calaf. And you?'

'What's that you say? Doctor? Doctor, God help us… and what fun you must have had getting it, eh?!'

The look on his face confirmed my suspicion. He was radiant with joy and embraced me around my midriff.

'Doctor!' I shouted, as if in need of some help.

'Ah, it's true,' said Armengol, standing up straight. 'And you? Tell me, tell me, what's your news?'

'Hold onto your hat and try not to fall over. You'll never guess what I've come to do! I've come… to buy a ring.'

Hearing this, Armengol jokingly stumbled backwards towards the wall with a look of shock on his face, dropped his arms and fell to his knees.

'I knew it!' he said, groggily. 'Don't say another word: it's that little Matilda, isn't it? My rival from your jaunts to Torralba.'

'The very same.'

'So, are you lovesick? Have you fallen for her?'

'What would you do? The Torralba air isn't any good for those who tend to suffer from these kinds of illnesses.'

With our eyes lit up, we linked arms as back in our university days and went to sit down at a table in the hotel restaurant to have lunch and to catch up. The conversation was flowing even before we opened the bottle of Champagne that Armengol had ordered in celebration. There was so much to talk about, not having seen each other for two of the most important years of our lives!

'Yes, man, yes,' I said, unfolding my napkin. 'They have us lined up in order of battle; the shooting has already begun. Luckily, one or two of us are still brave.'

'You, especially,' said Armengol, alluding to my wedding.

'We'll see what happens to you in a year's time, there in Plana-llonga. The mountain air arouses such heat in the blood that it can provoke heart attacks. I doubt that even you will be immune to it. After just six months, the pain will be such that you won't be able to move. Then nothing, you'll be trapped there, helping farmers, putting Spain to rights at the chemist's, worshipping the mayor's baton, and wearing the same bowler hat for ten years. Exactly what would happen to me if I decided to stay in Torralba.'

'So where will you go?' asked Armengol, pausing a moment before eating the food he had piled up on his fork.

'Look, the Carlists have done me a favour. My father is so sick to death of the shocks and unpleasantness that we've decided to come to live in Barcelona once I've done the *In nomine Patris et Filii et Spiritus Sancti. Amen.'*

'Goodness me! What a coincidence! I, too, plan on coming to live here with my mother… Well, let's have a drink… Let's toast, let's toast, this we have to celebrate!'

We told each other in detail about the projects we had undertaken in our lives, and I had to confess that, what with my father the way he was, I hadn't thought of anything else except marrying the girl who had stolen my heart. We then started, with a certain amount of sadness, to reminisce about the girls from Barcelona who we had once dated; our most cherished classmates, now all dispersed; and all those happy, tender, engaging or simply ridiculous moments that we'd had during those few happy, easy-going years together. And just when we started to get serious about the intimate things that we never spoke about, like the fact that the only really, truly sweet time in one's life was now well and truly behind us, we wiped our moustaches in silence and got up from the table. What do I know? We hadn't yet had enough.

It must have been the bittersweet tone that the conversation had taken on in the last hour that encouraged us to continue when, in the middle of that silent pause when we were both slowly putting on our coats, hats and gloves so as to stretch out the moment, Armengol turned to me with a look of great joy on his face.

'Wait, man, wait!' He exclaimed. 'I've forgotten to tell you about the *Bandereta*! How could I have forgotten! Come on, let's go for a stroll. I have a few things to do.'

'Yes, ok. I haven't heard anything about him since I went to Vilaniu. Do you remember what happened to us, my cousin and me, at his house?'

And so off we went up the Rambla, Armengol laughing as he so easily did as he continued to tell me the curious story about the man from Vilaniu who caused him so much mirth.

According to his sources, throughout the parliamentary sessions our hero had made sure that he was always to be found at General Prim's side. They had got to know each other, and he'd proceeded to visit him with a maddening idolatrous regularity that nobody but political leaders seem to know how to put up with. Contrary to what Adela imagined that day she gave us her sermon, her brother hadn't dared speak up even once in parliament. He would listen to Prim and his allies, open mouthed, almost drooling, before then voting for whatever they had proposed. Much in the same adoring way, it seemed to me, that his mother had no doubt spent days at a time before the Virgin, pleading with her to guide her husband back onto the right path. With but a few short breaks, he had spent almost two years like this at parliament, wasting away, abandoning his duties and the care of his sisters, and taking at face value what seemed to him to be an important patriotic sacrifice, but which was rather a puerile satisfaction of vanity. The people closest to him saw that the seven or eight times he had nodded his head in parliament and the relationships that he had struck up with the less disdainful members of the political establishment, had cost him not only money, but also the total collapse of his industrial business. What's worse, it had led to the total discredit of his elder sister who, enraged one day by her hunchback sister's tantrums, had disappeared for forty-eight hours with some local hunter.

It might be worth mentioning that when we got to these last, pitiful details, Armengol was far from amused. It's not that Serra-llonga had ever inspired in him any of the intense affection and, to a greater or lesser degree, admiration that only the cleverest or most excellent people ever earned from us, but at the very least he produced the kind of compassionate sympathy that is so often inspired by men like him, once you got to know them. On the other hand, few of the facts themselves were taken seriously, regardless of to whom they referred. Because of this, both of us launched ourselves into everybody else's moral considerations so that we might suppress them, and we thought back, with some sadness, to Giberga's previous predictions.

'Oh! Wait a minute, wait! The most alarming is yet to come!'

'You certainly have a lot of news, don't you?'

'And imagine what I've missed out! Just imagine how much gossip one could prise out of these kinds of people in four years! Well, if you don't mind, I'll continue. The monarchy votes and Prim is assassinated. Just imagine the body blow Serrallonga must have had! He says that in those moments he was in Vilaniu looking to patch up that which he would rather not admit to: basically his political organisation that he had to close down, and his sister Adela who he had to whisk off and hide in one of his country houses after beating her black and blue.'

'Goodness me!'

'And then, just as he was out of the way and busy dealing with these unpleasantries… boom! Prim is assassinated in Turco street! Such was his shock, as I said, that having posted off a telegram to the government and another, more tearful one, to the *condesa* of Reus, he collapsed and spent three days in bed!

'Poor old *Bandereta*! I told you, he has a good heart!'

'Wait, wait. Now you'll understand. Once he got over his despair, and goodness knows what he was thinking,' as he said this Armengol started laughing to such an extent that he found it difficult to continue. 'He went off to Madrid to look for revenge.'

'What the devil!?'

'He wants to avenge the death of his idol. "Nobody, nobody," he said, "would take on the task with such gusto as I would." And once there, he goes and tells a certain Calado, a scrounger who had been leeching off him for a while and in whom the poor man had placed his trust, all about his plans.'

'Oh dear, oh dear...'

'I know! The thing is that this Calado – maybe to further milk his cash cow, but at least to keep Daniel close enough to have a little fun with him – not only approves of the plan, but also promises to aid and abet its architect. Why? Who knows? And after many mysteries and forced promises, three or four fairy tales come to the fore that lead Daniel to believe that what happened in Turco street came from Rome, from the Jesuits, the greatest enemies of the House of Savoy. The very same people who had been seeking revenge against those who had brought a prince of that house to Spain. Well, in the end, a variety of unearthed clues all point to a priest living on Gorguera street.'

'Blimey...'

'That wise guy Calado sees that he has Serrallonga all tied up, doesn't he? Could you ever imagine anyone more gullible than Daniel? By then, Serrallonga's turmoil was in full flow. With his head about to explode, the poor wretch left the conference and by all accounts he was all over the place: he presented himself to the Countess, the ministers, even to the King himself acting as a special secret commission charged with chasing down and capturing General Prim's assassins, assuring everyone that he held the key to the plot and that he alone knew how to crack it. They all receive him, watching him as he arrives sweating profusely. They pretend to listen to the endless discourse he mounts – tears welling in his eyes – by which he hopes to convince them. And they clock him immediately and politely dispatch him with a "come back tomorrow, sir". The next day he goes back, and the next day, and the next, for weeks on end. All the while his spirit battles on, tossed between hopes now glimmering now dashed, all depending on the way the officials look at him, or the tone with which they talk to him when they receive him. He doesn't sleep, doesn't eat, doesn't relax, and spends all day chasing ministers around. Likewise the chief of the police, who now considers him suspicious either due to the hilarious excess of malice Daniel shows towards him and his workmates, or even because he's a little jealous. Daniel spends his time walking up and down Gorguera street again and again spying on the poor man who Calado convinced him to hire to watch over the imaginary priest's movements, and crying in desperation at the government's indecision that, at any moment, might frustrate his honourable intentions. Calado, meanwhile, is entertaining himself and living out of poor Serrallonga's pocket. A snake in the grass. What's more, what really sends Daniel mad, is that Calado apparently knows that, if the government is stalling, it's because it has sold out to the Jesuits.'

'Oh no, no, no!'

'That's the long and the short of it. And everything I've just told you comes from the very same Calado's mouth. Well, I don't want to bore you. The government, where suspicions against Serrallonga grow ever stronger due to his interminable concern and the lack of success on behalf of those who observe him, decide to find out what he knows. Serrallonga gives them nothing but goes on saying again and again that he knows "where the wolf lies, he lies in Madrid, he hasn't yet left". But he's already said too much, the poor man. His inquisitors have already sniffed out, in effect, the trail and they know that the assassins have not only crossed the border but are already halfway across the Atlantic on their way to the United States! And so, the minister looks closely at the man standing before him, smiles discreetly and, either moved by compassion or worried that he might laugh out loud, can't stop himself. "Come back tomorrow," he says. And the next day... Well, you can picture the scene. The minister receives him along with the chief of police and, patting him on the shoulder, they tell him in no uncertain terms that he get his head looked at. Serrallonga starts to turn white with rage. He's now certain that the government has sold out. His lips tremble. He's about to explode. But the minister isn't finished there. He whispers in Daniel's ear that he is neither to trust in any conspiracy theories nor to commit the imprudence of placing some poor soul in fancy dress on Gorguera street or anywhere else for that matter. He tells him that he shouldn't waste away his fortune on lazy conmen and that he most certainly should not pour scorn on his investiture as a Member of Parliament by being seen with people like that.'

'Oh, incredible! And what did he do then?'

'He went from white to red, started to smack himself about the forehead with the palm of his hand, stopped sharply and, slamming the door less than convincingly, said in a threatening voice: "I will get to the bottom of this! To the bottom of this!" Only the complete disappearance of Calado and his poor henchman, both of whom the police must have wanted to clap in irons, could convince Daniel of the ridiculous situation he found himself in in Madrid.'

'Poor chap!'

'Yes, but what do you think? Do you think that it all made sense to him? Come on, now! In just a few hours from now, and what's more seeing that Prim's killers are no closer to being caught... don't doubt for one second, he still thinks that the government is in on the whole thing.'

'Blimey! But everyone at least knows what started the plot. If they haven't been able to catch the ones who did it, it's simply because the means of extradition doesn't exist due to the delicate political situation! Who couldn't see that Calado was conning him? Where have the police got all this from?'

'This last point, yes. I've already told you that the police saw what was going on. But they didn't see the good faith shown by the government and the charitable sincerity with which the minister treated him. The most important thing for Daniel was to punish those who did the crime. No punishment has come about. As such, either the Jesuits have bought impunity for the assassins or, as they now say, supporters of the monarchy ordered Prim's death to get him out of the way. All this he believes to such an extent that afterwards he went to the republicans. He pulled out all the stops so as to take up his political position again. And, once finally back in parliament he let the supporters of the monarchy know full well what his thoughts were on what had happened during those last few days. So much so that neither his own side nor even the President himself could stop the raging bull. They say that he named very important names in the army, made libellous accusations against all and sundry and that, by blindly hitting out left and right with his cane, brought the Chamber to a standstill. They had to use force to make him stop and to remove him from the room.'

'Seriously?'

'I'm telling you. If you didn't spend such long hours with that little Matilda, you would have almost certainly seen something of it in the newspapers. According to my friend at the press conference, he was out of control, sublime, incomparable. And there I was in Madrid at the same time... I can't believe I didn't go! If I hear that Serrallonga is going to speak again, then I'll sell the shirt off my back to go and listen, believe me! I wish I'd been there!'

'But didn't you see him in Madrid?'

'I was supposed to! If only! It was just when I was writing my thesis and I only went out at night. When I heard news of the breakdown, I made straight for the conference room on the off-chance that the *Eternal Avenger* – as we'll have to call him from now on – was still there. But, alas, I arrived too late. One of his party members, still laughing as he spoke, assured me that he had already left Madrid, swearing as he went never to return unless at the head of a legion of torches "ready to burn Madrid to the ground and to wipe out, once and for all, the rot fermenting there". Afterwards they told me that while all this was going on, that little devil Adela, desperate to escape from Daniel's clutches, had broken the bars of the prison where he was keeping her. She had then escaped into the arms of some wanton bachelor from Vilaniu and married him. Some guy called Riudavets who had been chasing her for a while.

FIVE

My head was still overflowing from all the previous tragicomedy when later that night Armengol and I went to see *Els Hugonots* at the Liceu theatre. There, we bumped into Giberga, who had been working as a doctor in Vilaniu for the last three years.

'This afternoon,' said Armengol, the three of us having already greeted each other and made small talk, 'we were reminiscing about some friends from the glory days and you came up, along with the celebrated *Bandereta*, of whom no doubt you can give us some exciting news.'

'Ah, you mean Serrallonga!' laughed the doctor. 'I thought as much: it's exciting alright. That business in Madrid…'

'We already know all about what happened in Madrid,' I said. 'This one here filled me in this afternoon.'

'Well, back in Vilaniu, he was at home and determined to fully withdraw from public life. Adela needed a distraction and was lucky enough to snare an old man who was happy to take anything he could get. Thanks to him she has no need to have anything to do with her siblings, nor any care in the world. Daniel gave her the part of the inheritance that she was entitled to, and *pax vobis*.

Amongst all this coming and going, the fact that Daniel was able to offload a weight as heavy as that sister of his with such ease was very fortunate. But he was so on edge and so manic that I'm not sure he even realised what he was doing. All I know is that he spent months on end in his room, sprawled across his armchair, slovenly dressed and completely undone, only ever wearing slippers on his feet, his pipe hanging from his lips. Most likely going over and over the same idea, and only ever leaving his room to wander down to the dining room. He would sit with the hunchback without making any eye contact with her and eat quickly, his eyes fixed on his plate or on the baubles that hang on the blood-red walls. Meanwhile the hunchback, like a hyena, would pick her bones clean and crunch her breadcrusts, all the while spying on her brother out of the corner of her eye without uttering a single word. Once they had finished dessert, the terrified hyena would get down off her chair like some poor, infantile creature and would run off to hide in the most remote places in the house. More than four times now my father has had to go and find her in the throws of one of her epileptic fits. It's thanks to him that I know about all these things. With Carolina out of the way, her brother would drink his coffee alone, light up his pipe and pick his teeth. Leaving his napkin unfolded on the table he would then head off back to his usual hiding place having uttered only the most necessary of words to Margarida, the one servant they have left around the house.'

'What a devil!' we said in shocked unison as we bunched up into a corner of the corridor so that Giberga could continue his story in peace.

'One day, my father who, as you know, has always been their family doctor, was called up by Daniel himself, someone he hadn't seen for more than a year. Complaining of severe headaches and blurred vision, Daniel told my father that bright lights hurt his eyes, that he had lost his appetite, couldn't sleep and couldn't concentrate on anything because of the torment of a single idea that ran around his head day and night.

"It was bound to happen, with the life you lead!" shouted my father as he handed over a largely pointless prescription to the old woman, Margarida. "It's nothing, nothing. You have to pick yourself up off this easy chair, take your rifle and go off hunting or digging on your country estates, believe me."

"But sunlight hurts my eyes!" said Daniel.

"So put sunglasses on. It would just be for a few days."

"And these headaches? These pains?"

"They'll pass. This medicine I'm prescribing for you cures everything. Come on! Get out of here! This is what you need! Throw away your pipe and head out into the countryside. Enough of your solitude and silence: a rifle round your neck, a good friend and off you go. Come on lad, you can do it!"

It was as if someone had put a rocket up him. My father says that Daniel jumped out of his chair and landed in front of him with his eyes bulging out of his head. He then started to rant and rave like a madman, insulting my poor father who could hardly believe what was happening.

"If anyone should get out it's you, you idiot, you imposter!" screamed Serrallonga.

"But, Daniel, what are you saying?" replied my father.

"You can hear what I'm saying! And I take nothing back! You are an ignoramus, a nobody, an insignificant leech! Come here!"

"Come on now, lad… come now…" said my father, still not yet over the shock.

"I don't want to hear it, no "lad", or… or devil! What do you think you're playing at, sir? Do you think you're dealing with a simpleton, one of those idiots you exploit every day? Well, you're out of your depth now! I'm an engineer, do you hear? I'm a scientist, and I'm a hell of a lot smarter than you! I've rubbed shoulders with General Prim, do you hear? With the most important man of the whole century! Yes sir, century! For here and for the whole world! Do you hear?!... I've been to the palace, I've been a member of parliament, I've dealt with all of the ministers and generals, and I've hassled them all... because I am more worldly and more scientific and know more than you, Mister Tites! Yes! Mister Tites, Mister Tites, Mister Tites! You are nothing! Nothing!!"

"But come now, lad, calm yourself, for the love of God! Calm down!" shouted my father, shocked to see him in such an alarming state of agitation, obviously raving, despite him insisting he wasn't. But the patient, out of his mind, as white as a sheet, wouldn't stop staring at him and as my father retreated so Daniel advanced, pushing him towards the door.

"And yes!" continued Daniel, threateningly. "Don't you see, Mister Tites, what you are advising me to do? How do you want to cure me? With a wider world view? With contact with other people? The thing I hate the most, the thing I detest more than anything! Why don't you advise me, you idiot, to end it once and for all? Where is your science? What are your weapons, your arguments? Oh! Where are they, your fists, to force me to do your bidding?"

"Sir, I advise you. It's my duty and you called me!"

"And what do you know of your duties, you ignorant old codger? When have you ever dedicated yourself to your studies? When have you ever burnt the midnight oil as a student? What have you ever invented? What have you discovered? What knowledge do you have that you haven't found in books, without having even bothered to test them yourself?"

"Daniel, I'm leaving. I can't take this anymore."

"Ah! The truth hurts, doesn't it? Well, I'm going to tell everyone! That's that! I ask you for solace, for a curing balm, and what do you offer? The opposite! You prescribe a beating for an already bruised piece of meat, pleading to be cured. "I'm weak! I have no strength!" I tell you. And you reply: "walk, dig, wear yourself out". "My eyes sting! I can't stand bright lights!" I say. "Wear sunglasses," you reply so as not to say: "get out of here, you loon." I say: "My pipe makes me happy, it takes my mind off things. I'd miss it: I couldn't live without it!" "Throw it away immediately," you say. "I'm at home avoiding people because I'm bitter, because I dislike their company, because they remind me of piles of rotting meat and they make me sick to the stomach!" And you say, you idiot: "Oh! A rifle and a friend!" What will he make me do, this friend? You, creator of impositions, echoer of strange words, the meaning of which you've never even understood? Is this your science, you fool?"

It was evident that the melancholic voice of madness rolling around his head had entirely devoured him in his solitude. His egotism, false notion of self-worth and destiny on this Earth, and the vanity that, in effect, was the prelude to so much of his embryonic madness coupled with the disappointment of Madrid, had taken on the satanic proportions of hubris that, all too often, characterise the principal deliriums of these kinds of insanities. His pride had removed itself from the mortal domain. For him, all men were either foolish or evil. That said, they should never have imprisoned him for the Delícies incident or tricked, mocked and ridiculed him behind his back at parliament. As far as women were concerned, both the Adela situation and his unstable mental condition coincided to cause him to make some calamitous generalisations: he considered them all filthy, vicious and indecent. Apart from him, there was nothing pure, nothing intelligent and nothing honourable in the world. Society in general was a huge pile of manure, and not worth his time.

He continued abusing my father's patience in this vein for a good while. Yet my father still felt obliged to try and help him because of their long friendship and that peculiar sacrificial aspect of our profession that is so little recognised. And so it went on until Daniel, overwhelmed by physical exhaustion, his tongue wearied, fell back into his chair. Then my father, like a surgeon delicately using a scalpel to reach some nerve without causing harm, took his leave with heartfelt words delivered with utmost sweetness in the hope of reaching down to the moral sensibility that might still exist within that being. It was just as good a tactic as any other. Daniel's outburst hadn't been too wantonly terrible, and my father seemed to make the right decision.

"Don't you see who you're talking to? Come on. Look, look at me," said my father in a pleading voice. "The little hair that I have left has already turned white. You used to play with it when it was still black. Don't you know that I saw you being born? That I played with you on my lap, like a son, dozens of times? Don't you know how much affection your parents had for me? The trust they placed in me when it came to your life, your very life, you who they loved more than they loved themselves and who bravely fought to protect you when you had scarlet fever and, later, typhus? But what? You, little Daniel, you yourself told me about your father's problems. Didn't you see me enter your darkness like an angel of salvation? How many times did I leave his side for seven days and nights? He died, it's true. Oh, but who could have saved your father? You yourself told me, little Daniel: "You have worked miracles." It was when I had you in my arms and was drying the tears that no one else could wipe away."

Fortunately, the fog hadn't yet covered everything. There was still a crack in the clouds where a ray of light might pass. Serrallonga burst into tears and collapsed in front of the doctor. The ridiculous prescriptions, the showers, the food and the countryside all rolled away with the storm.'

'But do you think he'll go mad again?' asked Armengol, clearly troubled by the situation.

'Without a shadow of a doubt. It has to come back one of these days, I'm certain.'

'Well, there *are* cases…,' I dared to interject, referring to the cured cases of neurasthenia that I could recall.

'Don't fool yourself; there's no comparison. Daniel's case isn't neurasthenia exactly, as my father and all the older doctors would have you think, but rather congenital madness: he's had it since he was born. His mother was hysterical, his father showed so many signs that, as I said, he died insane. What could possibly be the fruit of this marriage? Genetics is a clearly defined cause. Analysis of these mental illnesses points towards it being one of the main causes. What else? He has an epileptic sister. Doesn't Adela's behaviour, with her erotic outbursts, suggest her to be unbalanced, as well? And Daniel, when have you ever seen him behave like a normal person?'

'Come now,' said Armengol, 'Daniel has had long periods without doing anything out of the ordinary. How many families have some epilepsy or illness in them without any of them going mad? Honestly, I think that in this field you doctors tend to go a little overboard. You look for perfect, almost imaginary men who, even if they did exist, would be incapable of doing anything worthwhile. Meanwhile, you all end up like Diogenes and his lantern, treating the rest of us like idiots.'

But the inflexible Giberga avoided the argument.

'And so what about this?' he continued, imperturbable as ever in his ideas. 'Right this moment, with this crisis overcome, what do you think he plans to do now? Well, listen to this. He wants to get married. Out of stubbornness, what's more. Nothing else.'

Here the two of us burst out laughing.

'Daniel's getting married? Who would want him? Out of stubbornness? How hilarious!' But so shocked were we by the news that at that moment we didn't fully grasp the gravity of it..

'Oh yes, this is another primary symptom. But the bell's ringing: I'll tell you about it later.'

On entering the theatre we split up but, as far as I was concerned, it would have been better not to have gone in at all. The music I had enjoyed so many times did absolutely nothing for me. With my thoughts focussed on Serrallonga's real-life misadventures, it was impossible for me to listen to unrealistic heroes and their fictions, regardless of how dramatic the singers were. The music was just another noise and washed over me superficially without touching me. Armengol, as distracted as ever, couldn't get the idea of Serrallonga marrying for stubbornness out of his head. It made him chuckle constantly and he occasionally nudged me with his elbow to remind me of the fact.

Once again in the corridor and even more curious, we squeezed up into the same place as before so as not to be bothered by the elbows of the people passing by. Giberga came over and made some cultured comments which I assume came from his study of music, before getting back to his story.

'So you see,' he continued. 'The hunting friend that my father suggested was a chap called Genís Argila, otherwise known as *Fura*. He's a farmer from Comellar, Daniel's most extensive property and about an hour away from Vilaniu. The holdings aren't so far away so as to be unconnected, but they are close enough to the forest so that they are practically crawling up the side of the Bondelit range. What's more, the fact that it's worked by the only farmer who Daniel has never fallen out with is why our dear friend decided to go there, following my father's advice. Now, Fura is the best sheepshearer in the whole of the Vall de Flors and is well versed in Daniel's sad story. He feels genuinely sorry for him. As such, he was very happy to play the part of the pleasant companion and to encourage and entertain Daniel with the very best repertoire of jokes and stories that he had, to never contradict him, to praise him often and to stay close to him. Effectively, to do everything to help Daniel that he and his family could. The first few days, however, were very difficult for all concerned. The hypochondria and headaches, both of which hadn't completely disappeared, made Daniel as surly, bad tempered and slovenly as Vilaniu itself. The natural light, brighter than it was in the town, overpowered him with or without sunglasses. Not smoking also left him on edge and so he wasn't in the mood for conversation or for climbing hills or even for abandoning the easy chair in his bedroom at the farm any more than when he was at his own home. I mean to say that the scenery was different, but the problems remained. Nothing more. But after two weeks things started to change. The medication had banished the pains; the food and fresh air had made him stronger; the absence of Carolina and his ancestral walls had washed the slate clean and eased the internal fury that had dominated his existence for so long. The cloud over him started rapidly to disappear and after two months of living in the middle of the countryside, getting a moderate amount of exercise, Daniel was a new man. So much so that while my father still wasn't completely over his shock from the day of the great outburst, he would have rejoiced at the way things were going. But… here comes the crunch. With Daniel having come this far, would you believe that he received an anonymous letter denouncing Salomè Argila, the farmer's unmarried daughter, and warning Daniel not to marry her? That said, whilst anonymous, it was pretty obvious that the person who had written the letter had clearly never even set eyes on the poor girl.'

'My goodness!' Armengol and I said in unison. 'What madness!'

'Perhaps you are beginning to catch on. Daniel guessed that the letter had come from his sisters and, seeing that their motives consisted of hoping to inherit his part of the family fortune should he die without a wife, and the vanity of not wishing to be associated with a poor family, he became furious.'

'That's the least he should have done,' I said.

'What idiots! Idiots!' said Armengol, laughing. 'But then what? And Daniel?'

'Here comes the really mad thing. What would anyone else have done in his place? Reject with distain the ridiculous, selfish notion? If you were so inclined, get angry for a short while before laughing about it? Good God! Laugh about it, investigate it further if you will? Perhaps talk to Carolina about it, right?'

'Oh yes. Because in the end these siblings love each other so much…,' I said in an assenting tone.

'Exactly!' added Armengol.

'Ha! Well not him. He failed immediately. Ever since the first letter, it's become ever more obvious from the other anonymous notes and the sisters' gossiping that it was them. But Daniel entrusted himself neither to God nor the Devil and, with a satanic laugh of mad pride, said to himself: "Hello, hello! You don't want this? Then this is what you'll get." And from that day on he paid more and more attention to the little peasant girl who, by the way, is very pretty, kind and docile. He started to woo her with such passion that Fura, ever the greedy farmer, pricked up his ears and took up the scent.'

'Of course!' cried Armengol. 'Fantastic! And now they're married, right?'

'No man, not yet! I told you they weren't.'

'Oh, but they're getting married, that's for sure!' replied Armengol. 'And what if they ask us to be groomsmen at the wedding? How we'd laugh!'

'Come on, man,' I said, sincerely.

'What, "man"? What's he got to lose? It would be her, if anything! As long as they both know what they're getting into, I don't see what the problem is.'

'Ah, but that's just the thing,' said Giberga. 'How do you know if the girl and her family know he's mad? His madness slips in and out amongst the crowd and she doesn't even realise it. While his hysterics are kept below the surface, he appears to be original, eccentric, extravagant, even fun.'

I looked on with a certain horror at the seriousness with which Giberga presented these arguments, fruit of an indomitable conviction. Even Armengol looked serious. If, in the end, and as Giberga had told us so many times before, madness comes from an injury to the brain, as evidenced through the autopsies of thousands of cases, on what authority would a couple of lawyers be able to refute it? Not even as members of a jury were we comparable to a Rossi or a Beccaria or as psychologists to an Alfred Fouillée to whom, needless to say, we compared very poorly, so could we try asking him to remove us from the multitude that he was talking about? Giberga, as far as his science was concerned, was the opposite to a knot in an old oak: he played the role of the consummate psychiatrist. He was ever quoting, in his favour, Guislain and I don't know who else, and we simply weren't able to counter him.

'The proof of what I'm telling you,' he continued, 'is that the girl has ended up infatuated with him. It's clear that money, ever the devil on the shoulders of consciences less firm, has swung her more easily than it once did Serrallonga's parents, but when would Daniel's mother, Engracieta, have ever said that her husband was going to die raving mad? The subject is so complicated, requires such a large amount of information, and needs such a finely tuned and educated perception that it will always escape the abilities of the poor, deficient layman. Knowing how much Fura loves his daughter, I would bet anything that despite him being blinded by the interest, he wouldn't ever give her away to Daniel if he thought it dangerous to do so. To say nothing of that naïve-spirited young girl who, at the end of the day, would never have dreamed of this happening to her.'

'Believe me,' he added in that unpleasantly pompous tone of his, 'in a situation such as this the girl and her family will do what ninety-nine per cent of reasonable people do. The person who wrote those anonymous letters is both dim-witted and naïve. But the real madman is the one who has decided to marry someone he has never been interested in: the sole purpose of which is to do the opposite of what the letters say. As far as I'm concerned, it's as clear as the morning sun. But you two carry on thinking that madmen aren't like this at all, that they are rather desperate idiots. Your criteria are quantitative: mine are qualitative.'

SIX

Three months later I was married. We moved to Barcelona and settled into a place on Fontanella street with my parents. This way, my
mother had a church nearby and my office wasn't too far from the
centre. Well, that at least was the official story for anyone who asked.
But whenever I looked around the little apartment, filled by my
parents with furniture of the very latest fashions, I felt completely out
of place. Poor souls, I thought. For a flat this fancy they could have
got one by the sea in Barceloneta or even on the Passeig de Gràcia!
And here I am with lawsuits few and far between!

And that wasn't all. Little Matilda and I were practically in-
separable, and we went everywhere together arm in arm. So much
so that the first client to approach me would no doubt have thought
that I was rather reluctant to work. Even the three or four letters that
I had sent in as many months were written with Matilda at my side!

'Come, Tilda,' I would say, grabbing her around her waist.

And she would open the screen door and lift up the hem of one
of her many new muslin housecoats so as not to *deflower the virginity*
of the floor tiles that my mother made sure stayed ever sparkling,
and would accompany me to my desk. Once there, I would sit down

in front of a piece of paper – snow-white against the jet black of my briefcase – and she would crouch down next to me. She would then place one elbow on the desk while running her other arm around my neck. Then, weighed down by that sweet encumbrance, I would start to write, and she would reward me with kisses for every compliment about her that appeared on the paper. If the letter was for her parents, she would want to write something afterwards and so I would sit back in the chair and she would sit on my lap. As she wrote, I would pretend to dictate silly things for her to write out, blow her curls away from the back of her neck or nudge her elbow, making her slip.

How could I have written out a lawsuit or charge in such a state? What if it were a divorce document? And how could I have possibly sat down with a young, beautiful client one-on-one like this? Little Matilda was crazy about me, and I was crazy about her. Once, relaxing, half asleep and holding each other's gaze like swords crossing for what seemed like ages, I said to her:

'Listen, darling, I have a friend, a doctor in Vilaniu. If he saw us like this, he would say that we were completely mad and that we should be packed off to the madhouse in Sant Boi.'

She gave one of her little laughs that brought out her delightful double chin.

'How silly!' she replied in her high-pitched voice.

We went back to crossing our sweet, heart-felt swords and she fell around my neck.

'Isn't this madness so much more sublime than all human wisdom put together?' I whispered in her ear.

'I love you,' she said, her sweet little eyes looking intently into mine. 'Don't worry about what others say.'

In a state as delirious as that, who could possible think of clients?

In fact, who needed clients?

We were blinded by happiness, indifferent to anything but tenderness and caresses. Our souls, having taken off into infinite lands, were so obsessed by our absolute, mutual communion that we had forgotten about everything else. We went about the house, up and down streets, to the theatre, everywhere like this. And so one day, wandering around the city in our cloud of happiness – I don't remember which street it was: I hadn't even looked – I felt a soft tapping on my shoulder. I turned my head and found myself presented with Armengol's smiling, affectionate face. It felt as if he had come crashing back down on our heads from another, long since abandoned, world. And it was true: from those kind eyes and the smile on his lips came a sense of affection for a long friendship and a sweet ringing in my heart that I couldn't ignore.

'Armengol!' I shouted, blinking rapidly as if dazzled. I introduced him to my wife – what a word! I couldn't believe I was saying it! – and as soon as he told us that he was now living in Barcelona, I invited him to lunch the day after next.

For privacy's sake, I will spare you the fears of derailment that this invitation awoke in my young wife's jealous heart. The long and the short of it is that these fears provoked a tenderness of the sort that can never be forgotten, regardless of how soppy it is. Who knows to what extent these women feel the intoxicating perfume of such things enveloping them? What I do know is that those tears of innocent jealousy tasted to me like the richest nectar of the gods.

At table, my friend was as charming as ever. He enthralled both my parents and Matilda. We spoke of the wars that were taking place around the country, of the difficulty of living outside cities during that time, and of the problems that these sorts of things meant for the towns and villages: everything that worried my parents and not their children. With his conversational material exhausted, my father addressed Armengol and me and consoled us for all of the problems these things would no doubt cause us, from the difficulties that we would come up against when making our way in Barcelona, to the consequent necessity to speed up and carve out a place for ourselves in the city as soon as possible. This in turn caused us both to reflect on the origin of our friendship and how it had gone from strength to strength throughout our studies.

'Speaking of which,' said Armengol. 'You will never guess who is wandering around Barcelona these days, arm in arm, like yourselves, with his bride! None other than Serrallonga.'

'Oh! Is he married now?' I asked, half embarrassed that I might be considered to be copying him in that sense.

'Yes, old chap! And without asking us to be best men!'

I burst out laughing as I thought back to previous conversations, reminding myself of what we had already spoken about.

'Have you seen him?'

'Yes.'

'And what's his wife like?'

'Oh! What a gossip!' said my mother, laughing as always at everything I did.

'Oh right! Of course!' added my wife.

'Well!' continued Armengol. 'It's just that we're dealing with a *sui generis* wedding. They got married out of stubbornness.'

Everyone laughed in disbelief, especially little Matilda, who found the whole thing impossible, scandalous and indecent.

'Tell us, tell us,' I said as the exclamations died down.

'She's a hapless brunette girl.'

'And does she dress as befitting a lady?'

'Yes, and it suits her. She's slim, timid and holds herself well. Do you know what I mean? She's the kind of girl who… might easily slip through the cracks.'

The image took my parents and little Matilda by surprise and they responded with those typical broad smiles that new comparisons so often provoke in those who don't understand them.

'Yes, well… if she's like that…,' said my mother.

'No, but she has nice eyes, a handsome face and a kind, modest expression that makes her more than tolerable.'

'Well then why didn't you start with that?' replied my mother, laughing. 'I didn't know what to think when I imagined her slipping through cracks…'

'Well, madam, she only appears to be one of those, if you know what I mean. I'm not sure it sits well with her.'

'Oh come on, old chap. You're painting us a portrait here,' said my father.

'She can't be too uncomfortable,' I said, simply.

'She looks wrung out like a dry tulip,' replied Armengol in a tone so serious that it made the others laugh. 'I think it's because of the hat she wears on her head.'

'He's given her a hat to wear?' I shouted. 'A hat!?'

'And not an insignificant one, no! Poor girl! It has more colours and trinkets than a fireworks display.'

The way my friend spoke caused so much hilarity that my father, mother and wife were all urging Armengol to continue, compelling him to explain where all this had come from. It didn't occur to anyone there that Daniel was mad: the most daring thing they labelled him with was strange or extravagant.

'And have you spoken to him about the wedding?' I asked after a while.

'I haven't yet had the chance. But I know everything that's gone on thanks to a letter from Giberga.'

'Oh! Do tell!'

'Well, basically, it was all very outrageous, like everything the *Great Avenger* does. Giberga says that with Daniel increasingly under pressure from his sisters' opposition, he intensified his wooing of the girl until it turned into love. Tragic, tragic love. So tragic was this love, in fact, that the farm girl, shocked at the blind, ever more frantic and biting attacks on her honour coming from her future sisters-in-law, wanted to go back on her word and cancel the wedding. Well, at this, Daniel went back to Vilaniu and forced the hunchback out of the house with a broom before beating Adela and her husband in the middle of the street. You can just imagine the scandal! Back at the farmhouse, he proceeded to threaten to shoot himself if, after these outrageous acts in the streets of Vilaniu, which he called "conclusive proof" of his love, Salomè didn't change her mind. Such was the scandal that Vilaniu split into two camps: one, convinced by the sisters' rumours and accusations, that fell on their side, and the other that supported Daniel. When Salomè's father and brother realised that the girl was going to be doomed and lost forever more if she declined, they persuaded her to say yes. And so Daniel, high on victory, decided on having the biggest, noisiest wedding he could.'

'Sweet mother of God!' exclaimed my mother between yelps of laughter. 'What a unique fellow!'

'Quite the character,' said my father in a tone of admiration.

'Be careful Giberga doesn't hear you!' I added.

From here on we discussed the good doctor's various notions before we all branded him somewhat exaggerated, including Armengol and me.

'According to that young man,' concluded my father who, being rather sickly, had a constant bad cough, 'anyone who is any kind of

a character should be in a psychiatric hospital. Blah, blah, blah...
and that's that. He's mad!'

It was as if I was hearing myself in my father's voice, that I had
in fact inherited my disdain for Giberga's ideas.

'So, did he have his noisy wedding?' asked little Matilda, by now
completely captivated by the story.

'He doesn't say, but what he does say is that it was quite a show.
Apparently, even the factory workers downed tools and there were
cheers and whistling along the route. Even inside the church there
was such a crowd of people that it felt like a market.'

'And how was she dressed, the withered tulip, as you call her?'
asked my mother, finding the story more and more entertaining.

'I wondered that too. It seems she was dressed all in white, like
someone from the upper class. She probably looked more like a wet
chicken.'

'Oh, come on now!' cried the women in protest at what they
perceived to be exaggeration by Armengol. 'She can't have been in
white, surely! Too much, too much!'

'In white, ladies. In white. That's what Giberga told me. And with
a garland of orange flowers, bought in Barcelona and everything.
What were they thinking?'

'Well, they wouldn't make a peasant girl from Torralba wear
white, that's for sure. How very thoughtless these people from Vilaniu are!' exclaimed little Matilda, ever enraptured by her little town.

'Ha, but can't you see that all of this was done out of stubbornness?'
said my mother, laughing. 'She's obviously rather docile, this girl. I'm
telling you! But the money is appreciated, isn't it?'

'Enough, enough, enough!' said my father, unable to believe that
the farmer wasn't interested in money.

'But what about Daniel's dreadful sisters? Didn't they do anything in the church?' I asked.

'I don't think they did anything in the church, but they did outside. It was wholly inconsiderate and, frankly, great fun! They say that when the wedding party passed in front of the brother-in-law's house where both of the sisters now live, they put a spinning dummy, a straw man and a telescope out on the balcony, as if they were waiting for the carnival to arrive.'

'Crikey!' we said in unison. 'Who would do such a thing!'

'Well they did, alright. They're mad!' shouted my father.

'Wicked women!' I agreed, thinking back to the bad experience with Carolina in her house and of all the false affection Adela had shown towards her brother. 'But that husband of hers must be half stupid to let his wife act the way she does!'

'Ha! Everybody says that she hits him,' replied Armengol.

'Sounds like he's done well for himself!' shouted my father.

'Please! You can't go on like some poor little girl who thinks that if her husband didn't hit her, it would mean indifference and, who knows, a lack of love on his part.'

'Oh, how terrible!' exclaimed my mother and little Matilda at the same time, both enthusiastically contemplating the situation.

'What I'm really interested in is the face Daniel must have made when he saw the dummy on the balcony,' said Armengol. 'The urge he must have had to go up to the house and attack all and sundry, starting with his idiotic brother-in-law!'

'Oh of course, that would have been perfect, the lion tamer there, oh yes!' I replied.

'I can just imagine him in the middle of the street, his hat pitched back onto the scruff of his neck, his spectacles on the end of his nose, tie done up to his ears and his frock coat undone, fighting with a group of farmers and that father-in-law of his, Fura, as they try to hold him back. And I can already hear the cheers and whistles coming from the locals, and the bride's powerful voice as she shouts out: "Disgraces!" And I can see the two sisters laughing and clapping, their demonic faces looking out from the crack in the blinds they are spying from. And it's upsetting not to have been there. It would have been wonderful!'

'What nerve!' said my mother, by then crying with laughter. 'Stop, stop! I can't take anymore!'

'But you think it's all a joke! Can't you see that it's actually very sad?' said my father, wiping the tears out of his eyes.

'Sad? Sad? It depends on how you look at it,' stuttered Armengol with such seriousness that it made us laugh even more. 'What do you want me to say?' he added. 'I like this Serrallonga even more than the one from the legend. He's stolen my affections and I can't do anything about it.'

'You've been having fun with him for years now,' I said.

'Oh yes, oh yes. And long may it continue. How could you wish for a cheaper, more innocent form of entertainment?'

'I see that you're a man after my own heart: with but a little, you have all you need,' said my mother.

'Ah, yes madam, yes. And what more could you want from the world?'

Both my friend and my mother looked at each other and burst out laughing again, as if laughing at themselves and the childish genius that they shared.

SEVEN

About six years must have passed without hearing anything about Serrallonga, not even from the ubiquitous Armengol. Then, one morning I was in the hallway kissing my children goodbye before they went for a walk with their governess when a nervous knocking at the door led me to open it. A tall, thin, bearded man with very thick spectacles took off his huge felt hat and asked for the owner of the house.

'Please come in,' I said, hurriedly opening the room divider to the office before leaving him for a moment.

'Who is he?' asked Matilda as she came out of the reception.

'I don't know. He must have a lawsuit or something.'

'Well, be careful, you! What eyes! What a cane! What a tie!'

I smiled to reassure her and, kissing my children once again, I went into the office.

The stranger was staring at a photograph of the Law Faculty graduates taken in the last year of my degree. He was clearly short-sighted and to see the photograph properly the man had to stand right up against the wall in front of him where the photograph was. Because of this, he had his back turned as I entered the room. With the rug softening the sound of my footsteps, I took the opportunity to observe him for a moment. There was no doubt that I recognised him, but I wasn't sure who he was. Regardless, I went over to my table and settled into my armchair.

'What can I do for you?' I asked.

The man's shoulders trembled slightly and he turned around, walking over to me with cautious steps. Putting his hands on the other side of the desk, he leant forward to better cast his impertinent, inquisitive eye over me.

'You've certainly changed' he said, finally. 'I didn't recognise you when I first came in. Compared with your portrait on the wall. And me… Well, don't you recognise me?' he asked, almost certainly noticing the growing disquiet moving across my face.

'Tell me,' I said, mechanically.

'I'm Daniel Serrallonga, old chap!'

'Ah, of course. How are you?' I said coldly, still not recognising him. He was so thin, so faded, so very wrinkled. 'Your hair, your beard, many years have passed, you know.'

Quite apart from the white, hemp-like beard that he wore halfway down his chest, he had let his remaining hair grow long and wild around the prominent bald spot on the top of his head.

'Yes, just like you with that moustache and your Austrian sideburns.'

And he just stared at me and laughed with an affectionate expression of old friendship.

I then asked him to take a seat in front of me and offered him my hand like a good friend.

'Do you remember the Ciutadella incident?' he asked quickly, looking languidly up at the ceiling.

'But of course,' I said.

'How… very vague… I mean… how very long ago, those days! And how many days have since passed since… since… since that… what's it called… predicament!' He stopped for a moment, as if about to tell me something. But I could see on his face that he thought better of it. A look of sublime disdain appeared on his lips, and he continued to talk with the same silences as before but now somewhat more directly. 'I accept whatever battle that might present itself to me, and I maintain myself by laughing about it. I don't intend to get involved in anything.'

'Quite right. It's how all of us should go about our lives,' I said, moved to compassion by the bitterness with which he uttered his futile, all too obvious, boasts. Just like any other man might.

'You see… you see? I come to you with a lawsuit that I lost in Vilaniu… and it's all the same to me. The judge, a simpleton, a pain in the backside, a good-for-nothing, a… a… a… nobody, you know? He played a dirty trick on me, the wretch… but… look… worse than him! You, here, you could punish… you could hit… you could give him a wrap on the knuckles, it's the least he deserves.'

He then explained the situation to me. His sisters were disputing their father, Ignasi's, last will and testament in which he had named his son as his rightful heir. This was all, of course, simply to obtain an increase in the inheritance that Daniel had already taken for himself. The lawsuit hoped to nullify the act by showing that Ignasi had had dementia for many years before his death, proof of which was his treatment of his wife, doubts between friends of his fatherhood, his addiction to gambling and, finally, his suicide.

They were more or less the same premises that Giberga had used, many years ago, to try to bring us to the same conclusion. And pondering the coincidence, I trembled from head to toe at the harm that language can cause, even when used without malice. Because it seemed impossible to me that a man as honourable and discreet as Giberga could assist in any other way a lawsuit as daring and monstrous. He had shared his observations, based on scientific proof, with us during one of those discussions that one has as a young man. But due to the personal petulance of age and the blind credulity with which, back then, all things were believed, even the greatest absurdities were warmly accepted as truth. But would they be upheld today as exact and conclusive as they were then? Who wouldn't have been surprised when Daniel assured me that our friend, in open opposition to his father, had reached that judgement? Where is, therefore, the fine line between sanity and insanity? I was incapable of understanding how an opinion as reflexive as that young man's could be so roundly accepted despite its not having been read anywhere except for essentially materialistic, "progressive" journals. His convictions should have been well rooted in fact by contrary people, not necessarily myself, but rather by expert doctors. As they weren't, they seemed to me to be a falsehood and I found myself trusting less than ever in the judicial system.

'What are you talking about, man?' I asked, showing my surprise. 'I know Giberga. Did he interfere in this?'

'An... an... interference, yes sir, because his father had been the family doctor for such a long time. But it's not surprising, not surprising at all,' continued Serrallonga, staring pointedly at me and smiling. 'You obviously don't know that young man well enough. Now he, he *is* mad!'

And here he burst out into a laugh so broken, so cracked and so strange that it frightened me.

'Picture it, yes... all of it... how it must have been, what he dared to say I am and what my sisters are... those... those... who set about helping. It reminds me of what they say, about the chap in the asylum… you know?… the nurse that always found problems in what other people did. But that was only because he held himself in such high esteem that anything they did was unworthy.'

He burst out laughing again and waited for my approval. Yet all the while I felt confused, somewhat strange and sad all at the same time.

'And so who was it who opened the lawsuit?' I asked, worried that if I didn't get things back to the point, even I might lose my mind.

'Oh!… Pons, man, Pons!… a puppet… a… a mischievous fellow, an enemy of mine. That great friend of mine… Adela's man. The one who got married… with the… only problem being that… that he died.' As he got to this last part, Daniel laughed out loud.

'Well,' I said, trying to keep the conversation from veering off course. 'And didn't you then ask the sisters to withdraw the lawsuit?'

'Of course. And they pressed forward with it.'

He looked at me square in the face as I shuddered at the thought of daughters being capable of injuring the memory of their father so much.

'Ah, bah!' he exclaimed, finding, in the heat of his hatred, a greater force of words. 'As if you don't know who they are, that pair of adders! I know, of course… that one day you met them at the house, when they were rather impolite to you. Then the elder hag, since you let her get 'clever' with you, started sucking up to me and told me everything. But later, what with her being as self-obsessed and brazen as the younger one, she's since messed me about in every way possible. My father's inheritance! Can you imagine! He left her, net, a little house in Igualada that I sold when I liquidated the association I had set up before going to Madrid as a Member of Parliament. I got three thousand *duros* for it, was weak enough to give them five hundred each and look how they repaid me.' He let out another strange laugh and continued. 'Ah, but you haven't heard it all! If only you knew how much they have taken from me! When the elder one got married to that buffoon of... of a husband who died two years ago, she took the furniture, curtains and all the linen, half the house. And when the little one left me to go and live with her sister, she took the other half. I gave them both their part of our mother's inheritance, and still they would have given me problems if, being a bachelor back then and looking for trouble, Adela's husband, who would tremble like a leaf to my face, hadn't managed to get them to sign the waiver I had asked for.'

'And you are married now, am I right?' I enquired.

'Yes sir... and I'm a father. I have an heir. And this is where all their fury towards me comes from. To see me... like that... with... with a successor. Damn it! How it drives them mad! If they could kill the poor child, believe me, believe me that they would. Oh, if you knew what they do when they see him! My... my... my wife doesn't even dare to take him out the house. "Get out of here!" I say. "Give me the boy. No need for those dis... those disgraces to kill him if we keep him locked up and suffocating in here with no air!" And I take him out and we walk past the front of the Riudavets house, where they have their lair now. Ah! If... if they're out on the balcony! I see them up there! They either spit down in rage and disappear or, half hidden behind an open blind, they turn around, lift up their skirts and, well, you can imagine the rest. One day I was walking down their street looking for some boys to do some work for me. So blinded by their rage towards me were they that they didn't see the boys and, when they saw me and pulled up their skirts, I shouted: "Look, look, the moon!" Oh, how they ran off then!'

Despite the evident tragedy, I let out a chuckle and Daniel, far from being offended, started to laugh as well.

'Exactly, old chap. You have to look at it like that,' he added. 'If not, one would have to start beating them every other time, and my hands are already tired from all of that.'

'What? Have you hit them? Come on, now, no. Don't ever do that,' I advised him for his own good, knowing that the fewer people to know about his violent tendencies, the better.

'Have I beaten them? Ha! I've lost count of the number of canes I've broken across their ribs! But there's no other remedy, and not even this one is enough! Right now, when they… they jeer at me like that, the only thing that saves their skin is that their front door is locked. Otherwise they wouldn't do it! I promise you!'

'Well, no. You shouldn't do that, Daniel; don't do it. It would be better if you took it all like you said before: with a pinch of salt.'

'Oh yes! I take it all with a pinch of salt! How I laugh about it! The children run off screaming and telling everyone about it. That way the whole town finds out… which is what I want.'

'So you can see that that is quite enough punishment and, should a scandal arise, perhaps it's even a little too harsh!'

'Ha! You just watch and see how they react! You don't know them at all. And if I were to tell you that they had dared to besmirch our porch? Walking by wearing hats and whatever else, in the street? Ha! If I were to get my hands on them, you'd see how white I'd turn their faces! We'll get there eventually, mark my words!'

'Serrallonga, for the love of God, no! In no way! You have to take the higher ground… you should consider them…'

'Consider them what?' he jumped in, 'women they are not, you know? They are worse than animals! You have to understand that they have tried to make out that I am mad… ma… mad as a hatter! And I'm not joking! You should know that before I got married,

married because they didn't want me to, they tried to have me incapacitated! Lucky that we had that other judge! And did you know that they caused so many problems between my father-in-law and me that I was forced to cut back trees in Comellar to make up with him! My wife is terrified, petrified by them. So much so that she doesn't even want to go out of the house with me on the off-chance that we bump into them!'

'Ok, so do this. The first thing to do is to settle things down at home. Leave Vilaniu: come and live here.'

'What now? Of course not! That is exactly what they want. They want to be able to say that they've beaten me. Now more resolute than ever! Ha! There, well dug in… Let's see who… who can… who can last longer.'

'But come on now! It's just that…'

'Enough! Get that out of your head: it will never happen. Should I, the avenger of the victims of the police state; Prim's close friend; the man who… who… created the greatest scandal in the history of Parliament… should I bow down to those two snakes? How little you know me! I enjoy the fight! I was born for it! Look, if… that… if I ended up married to who I am married to, then they are to blame. They anonymously crucified me. Nothing was off the table… the tricks they played to… to… upset the wedding. They defamed the bride, they formed a group that mocked even me, they turned their backs on that… on my wife. Ha!… "Oh, you poor souls," I said back then to everybody on whom I would have to seek my revenge: tenants, clients, debtors. And I threw them all out of my properties and banned them without mercy. In one month, I started thirty lawsuits for the evictions. One a day, just like that… slowly but surely. Ha! They were cowering then, oh yes, and they haven't been back!'

'In any case,' I said, 'it's a great pity that you have had to live like this. Starting lawsuits is very expensive and… very unpleasant. Providing space between the two parties, however, would end it all.'

'Ha, no sir, no! As I've said, now more resolute than ever! The more they do, the worse it will be for them. Lawsuits fulfil me: their cost is the least of my worries. With what is up for grabs, even should I lose them I have caused enough anger so that I will always, always happily pay up, even if it comes to selling the shirt off my back!'

'Oh! But you must think of your family! You have a son! You could have more.'

What had I said? He got half up off the chair, leaned back over me and stared at me with unfocussed, half-glazed eyes.

'Were it not for this,' he said, solemnly, 'I would already have done what I have to do!' And, tapping his index finger on the tip of his now pale white nose as if sharing a secret with me, he added: 'One way or another, I would have found the method by which I would have brought them all together at the same time; my sisters, the lawyer, the two doctors and the witnesses and, once they were there, I would have roasted them all alive. Believe me, believe me!'

'Well think of your children,' I said in horror, seeing for the first time the madman before me.

At first, I thought of nothing but cutting the conversation short and asking him to leave the house. But then I resolved to call on all of my ingenuity so as to help him to win his lawsuit without adding to the turmoil in his head, like so many others had done through malice, jests or ignorance.

EIGHT

During the three years that followed, there wasn't a month that went by without Daniel passing by our house. He came first for a lawsuit and, with that won, looked for even the most minor excuse to drop in as he took advantage of his visits to Barcelona to look after the stocks and shares he had acquired during the height of the gold fever that was sweeping through the city at the time.

The happiness I brought him through my judicial victories first in Barcelona and then in Madrid, where he sent me to defend him whether I wanted to or not, provided me with evidence of the tension that his own self-worth must have been under throughout the fight. It also illustrated the great affection that I earned from him in triumph. From that moment on, he considered me to be the greatest lawyer in the world, a kind of Prim within the Spanish legal system. In addition to the honours that he paid me, all the while telling me that I charged too little, he gave me wonderful little extras. With every upturn he had on the stock market, he would shower me with gifts for my children and, at Serrallonga's rather forceful request, I twice had to dress up in my university gown and mortarboard to be photographed. He then had both photographs framed in grandiose style before sending one to me at my house and taking the other one to Vilaniu to place on the altar to his 'gods'.

There were, however, moments when such delirium tired me out and his impertinence made me nervous. At the end of the day, to revoke a sentence as unjust as that one wasn't worth any merit at all and so such extreme admiration felt ridiculous to me. This mockery caused me great embarrassment, but I had to swallow it *velis nolis* so as to not to appear churlish. Yet there were also relaxing, serene times, when I saw more clearly where his admiration came from. Oh, poor Serrallonga! It almost moved me. The unhappy wretch had always acted in the same way. He had always gone marching around with blinkers on, rudderless, attacking or retreating depending on the direction of the waves that violently pushed or pulled him all around.

All the dreams and deliriums that the stock market period brought about empowered him in most shocking ways. Would it be immodest of me to say that, had he not had me by his side, he would have ruined his family? If only to line his pockets with papers and live for the heady sensations of the game, how many more properties would he have sold in addition to the ones that he already had before I stayed his hand? Why, only to buy shares in the Vilaniu Railway Committee did he rid himself of two magnificent farmhouses and, if in those days the property at Comellar didn't go the same way, it was almost certainly thanks to Fura's influence, who still lived there. Alone, however, he would have done quite unthinkable things. This idea of making thousands and thousands of *duros* in one day, despite possibly losing them the next, truly entertained him, fitted in admirably with his tumultuous imagination, with the vibrant nervousness of his spirit, with the special charm that he had for the fight, and with the blind confidence that a vain man like that has in himself.

So, I struggled to stay his hand by making him see that the financial bubble couldn't last, and that, in the end, the more one put in, the sooner and harder it would all collapse. Yet he would just laugh at my fears and confess that, just like Prim before him, he believed in "death or glory" and assured me that one day he would be a millionaire. But, of course, the crash arrived and, like so many others, he had his fingers badly burnt. This injury to his self-esteem, I assume, led to him never stepping foot in my house ever again.

Two more years had passed without seeing or hearing anything from Daniel, when one splendid afternoon in June I was strolling through the Ciutadella park with Armengol, who I hadn't seen for a few days on account of him feeling a little under the weather. I was reminded of the *Great Avenger* and his stay in the prison that had once stood on the area now occupied by the gardens we were walking in.

'Ah, of course!' my friend cried. 'Didn't you tell me a few days ago that you hadn't seen or heard anything else about *Bandereta*? Well, have I got news for you, and hot news at that!'

'Have you seen him, perhaps?' I asked.

'Not him. Her. By the way, you knew that I had seen her when she was a bride, right? A little strange, cold, but acceptable? Well, when she stepped into my office the other day, she looked like an old woman. I didn't even recognise her. She sat down in my armchair with a veil over her face and one could make out only two jet black braids of hair on either side of her forehead. On her right-hand side was her skinny, pale son who looked and acted as if no older than an altar boy.' By now, Armengol was not speaking in jest, but in a very serious tone indeed.

'Poor woman!' I said. 'She must have suffered a martyr's fate.'

'Exactly. Listen. The woman had come to see the lawyer. When I told her who I was and expressed my surprise that she hadn't gone to see you, as you were her husband's councillor, she told me, dabbing the tears from her eyes with an already damp handkerchief, that she had come to start legal proceedings against her husband and that, as such, you wouldn't accept...'

'What? A divorce?'

'Exactly that.'

'What the hell, Daniel! Now I'm sure that...'

'Oh yes! Now I see it clearly. He's mad, mad! Listening to that woman, the number of times that I was reminded of Giberga inspired reverence towards the man, almost admiration! It would seem, my friend, that that doctor has a good eye for these things.'

'So, what's he done now?' I asked pointedly.

'Well! He's practically finished! They'll have to lock him away soon. There's no other option! And because of this I advised against the lawsuit that she was going to ask for, and I begged patience and caution while we waited to see what would happen.'

'Good!' I said, pleased with my friend's decision.

'Oh! But how she must suffer, that poor woman! Can you believe that she confessed to me that, having got married in fear, on the very same wedding night, once nothing could be done about it, her fears became very terrible realities. "Then," she told me, "I knew I was lost. I spent the night in tears." According to her, she sensed a great nervousness in him from his sisters' jeering that morning and so she tried to calm him down by caressing him, talking to him, putting into practise the plan that the girl had come up with to soften up his character, the plan in which lay all of her hopes when she decided to obey her father and marry the man. But you see that Daniel and his constant arrogance and blind rage took the poor bride's requests to be shameful attempts to dominate him and flew off the handle to such as extent that he ended up slapping her hard across the face. The poor girl, so severely and utterly disappointed, has never got over it. "I saw only three paths to follow," she told me. "Kill him, kill myself, or put up with the situation. And I decided on the last one, entrusting myself to the care of the Virgin.'"

'I understand,' I said. 'Because if she went back to her father, the madman would think that it was all Fura's fault.'

'And if you think about it, Fura deserved all he got. Come on! Anyone with a daughter would do well to never forget this!'

'Poor girl. You can see why she's so timid. And after that?'

'Well, faced with his wife's lamb-like humility, though perhaps also because the cloud lifted like it has so many other times, it would seem that Daniel not only regretted what he had done, but even found himself truly loving the poor woman up until just a few months ago. I reckon that the change must be a result of the battles, with both his sisters and the stock market, finally coming to an end. With both of those issues out of the way and the rough waters from before now as calm as a millpond, he's gone back to his old ways. He spends his time sprawled out in his easy chair, frets constantly and is bad tempered for weeks on end. His wife manages to get him to leave the house for the occasional stroll and tries to cheer him up by engaging him in conversation. One day, they had just got home from a walk and she's taking off her veil while Daniel is locking the door behind them when "with those eyes, those eyes!" as she calls them – terrified even to mention them – he stands in front of her and grabs her arms with his talons. Then, with his face by that point completely changed, he demands to know why she had made him leave the house. "Oh! Oh!" says the woman in pain, surprised to find herself standing before the despot from their first night together who, thank God, had until that moment disappeared. "Can't you see? Have we not been together?… We went out for a walk." He tightens his grip until she is wailing and screaming. "Liar! Deceiver! Liar!" he shouts. "We went out because you wanted to… to see your fancy man!'"

'Now he's jealous? I said. Oh, poor woman!… And who is he jealous of?'

Here Armengol burst out laughing. He couldn't take it anymore.

'You'll never guess. He suspects… Giberga.'

So broken, so ridiculously absurd was the suspicion to anyone who knew Giberga's arrogant ideas and opinions that one just had to laugh out loud. Giberga? Interested in a peasant girl dressed up as a lady, as thin and pallid as an altar statue? Giberga, lover of all things lush and robust, fine food and silks, going after a strange girl without any attractive qualities apart from a good, albeit crushed spirit? Even I laughed out loud.

'Oh! It's just horrendous, horrendous! These things could only happen to *Bandereta*!' said my friend, catching his breath. 'And well,' he continued, this time in a more serious tone, 'from that terrible moment onwards, how much injustice and shock have the woman and the child, once the apple of Daniel's eye, had to suffer? All manner of infernal torments ferment beneath the deathly silence of that house. Poor Salomè can't step foot in the street, have friends over or even lift up the lace curtain to the balcony. That red-bearded, grey-eyed Othello spends all day silently prowling around the house with his sharpened nails, ready to maul anyone he comes across. If ever he leaves the building, it's under false pretences of remorse and is only to patrol the town, looking for the lover's shadow that he sees crawling up and down the walls and under the beds, everywhere. And he opens and rummages through everything and shouts and attacks any innocent comments that might come from all and sundry.

Oh! And when he rummaged through one of the wardrobes! How terribly it pained him! He confined himself to his single bed. That's another thing: he has slept alone now for a long time because he is bored of her. What a contradiction! He doesn't take his eye off her for one minute! Worst of all, she says that in the middle of the night he wakes, jumps up, and sets off like a bullet towards the quiet alcove where Salomè is with the boy and, brandishing a knife in his right hand and a wooden paddle in his left, shouts "Aha! I have you now! I have you now!" The two poor souls are sleeping, if not peacefully as is deserving of honourable people, but wrapped up in innocent embrace, under cover of darkness. Daniel, despite this, hears whispering and even loving words uttered. And as he gets closer, he thinks he sees a light and a sliver of some shadow dancing on the wall and the outline of the toilet door darken. The woman and her child wake up terrified. They beg him, they get on their knees, they plead. He brandishes the knife and beats, insults and threatens them, looks again under the beds, behind the curtains and inside the wardrobes, upending everything onto the floor.'

'Oh dear, oh dear. Those poor people!'

'Oh yes! As I said, it's just terrible. Oh, and listen to this: there's more. Once or twice, unable to sleep, he has confused Salomè with a burglar who he thinks got into her bed as he was trying to escape. With his claws around her neck, he almost kills her before leaving her for dead. The child's terrified screams then lead him back to where his wife is lying. Recognising her again, he breaks down in tears and ventures out onto the balcony shouting for help. The neighbours have to come and enter the sacred alcove and witness the terrible scenes.'

'But can't the doctor see what's going on? Doesn't he do anything?'

'And here's another one of the poor woman's lawsuits. With an extraordinary level of common sense, the woman sent for a different doctor who wouldn't remind her husband of Giberga in a million years. But little help did that do. What can I say? It was worse. Daniel accused the new doctor of poisoning him and of being in league with his wife to make him disappear.'

'Jesus, Mary and Joseph! It's beyond the Pale!'

'Didn't I tell you? It's a case for the psychiatric ward. This man is suffering from complete paranoid delirium. As such, any judicial action that puts him in prison is not only rash, but cruel.'

'But this poor woman is fearing for her life! A madman like this could well kill her one day!'

'And this is why she has taken precautions. She now has her brother at her side and, thanks to this and the fact that Daniel has been a bit out of it for the last few days, she was able to escape to Barcelona.'

'And did she tell you where this new frenzy of Daniel's came from? Did he lose a lot on the stock market?'

'We spoke about it and, well, she isn't stupid, in any sense of the word. "Yes," she said. "The greatest treasure that he could have lost, the illusion of being rich, the last sunflower to have bloomed in his garden." What do you think of that? Until now, this woman had never considered him to be mad. In Vilaniu, they still can't see it. Those who had been witness to the terrible night-time dramas rather suspect her. Can you believe it!? The mildest theories continue to maintain that which has always been at least partly true: that Serrallonga likes to drink. Nobody actually says he's mad, apart from the two doctors, but they also once said that his father was. The others, beginning with Giberga Senior and ending with the last person to visit him, are of a different opinion. They give it only passing importance. Carolina, the hunchback, says that her brother has poison flowing through his body, and you can already guess at who she thinks is responsible.'

'And Adela?' I asked.

'I suppose that she says much the same... if she says anything at all. Because I'm sure you know, now that her husband is dead, that Adela now lives with Mr Pons, the lawyer who served the first lawsuit.'

'What devils! What a family! But what do they live on, she and Pons?'

'Oh, her money. He doesn't do anything and seems to be having a whale of a time.'

'Goodness me! So, what about Carolina? Does she also live with them?'

'No, she still lives up in the house with the old servant, the only person who can put up with her stupidity and is charitable enough to care for her.'

We found ourselves heading up towards Barcelona's towering Columbus statue and our conversation digressed slightly as we talked about the delightful temperature at that time of the afternoon between the palm trees and the salty freshness of the sea air. Yet the subject quickly got back to talking about Serrallonga and Giberga, the latter of whom I considered to be in immediate danger of suffering at the hands of the former.

'What do you mean?' asked Armengol with a laugh. 'Because he's jealous?'

'No, Armengol, no. Don't laugh. I see this ridiculous, unfounded jealousy as a product of some kind of chronic sadness. Poor Daniel doesn't realise, but it seems clear to me. Giberga has pronounced him mad, in passing, but he bases this on an investigation of that same incapacity that I spoke to you about. What's more, Giberga provided Pons with arguments regarding his miserable lawsuit. As such, as far as Daniel is concerned, the figure of Giberga, and don't doubt it for one second, has taken on the rôle of an unpleasant and tireless persecutor, a traitorous robber of his happiness. Oh! And Giberga understands little of the humanity and misery of these sick people, who we ought to be treating like fragile flowers, in their honour and as our sacred duty! Don't you doubt it! I don't know if there is an injury, as Giberga assumes, or not. The doctors and those who ought to know don't understand the cause, or etiology as he calls it, of mental illness; or perhaps they do. I haven't the foggiest, but it doesn't seem possible to me. It's a mystery as deep and unfathomable as the essence and function of reason itself. And when I wonder about all this and see that even the simplest precautions within this whole mysterious order are seriously lacking, it shocks me to see how both wise men and fools treat these fragile brains. How often do I regret what we did to poor Daniel, when we were but 'children', when he was locked up in the Ciutadella! Aren't we at least partly to blame for the disaster that we're talking about?'

'Wait, wait a minute! What was our intention?'

'I was coming to that. Whether meaning to or not, but always with cruel intentions, starting with family members and finishing with the last boy in the street, society as a whole pushes and throws down into those communal graves of living flesh, that we call insane asylums, some ninety percent of those who suffer from mental illness. And it's terrible, Armengol! Here you have our case, for example. His sisters' behaviour, Giberga's, too.'

'His sisters? But can't you see? They're as mad as he is!'

'Cruelty and wrongdoing can easily be confused with madness when not studied closely. And Giberga, if he really is on the ball, if he knows as much about psychology as he thinks he does, if he doesn't deny the influence that emotions and moral causes must have on reason, then how, how can he truly quantify his behaviour? What kind of conversations must they have had to encourage such an illness?'

'Oh, but come on! He was speaking scientifically. Would you dismiss any opposing opinions when it comes to law, so that he who was wrong might end up ruined? You have always been sentimental but, frankly, today you're...'

Armengol was cut off by a great amount of shouting and a number of people running from a pile up in the middle of the avenue. We ran over to see what it was. Little rascals, like rabbits out of their warrens, were escaping out through the gaps made by the shrieking adults and as we ran over we almost knocked a few over.

'What is it? What is it?'

'Ha! A crazy man,' someone told us, smiling.

As one would expect in that situation, my heart jumped. The tumult of people there represented a palpable example of what I had been saying just moments before. Armengol and I moved through the compact mass of the playful multitude, pushing, shoving and elbowing our way through.

It seemed as if we were never going to make it. Or rather: thank God that we did!

In the middle of the ruckus was a very tall man with a pale, distorted face and greying, ginger hair who, half dazed, tie-less and with a straw hat balanced on his head, was looking up into the sky with a face as grey as his hair. He raised his cane above his head, shouting incoherently about invisible ghosts before suddenly starting to hit out left and right. The shouting increased and the air itself seemed to whistle. Following the outburst, the crowd celebrated having avoided the flailing stick in a rapid, instinctive motion with idiotic, scandalous laughter. Meanwhile, the 'madman' was trapped within the circle. No two seconds passed without some of the more insolent members of the group trying to interrupt the poor wretch's shouts by yanking on his jacket, pinching his leg, throwing mud at his hat or threatening him with a cane.

When we realised that the victim of those savages was none other than poor Serrallonga, our first reaction was to start to beat all and sundry with our own canes, and not blindly either; rather upright and across the middle of their heads in the hope that the blows might ignite some kind of conscience within them. I seem to recollect brandishing my cane above someone as if to thrash him but my friend, cooler than I was, warned me of the danger we were in and so I went off to alert two policemen who were lazing around further down the avenue, as they so often do. Meanwhile, Armengol went to hail an empty taxicab. On the same avenue was an aid station, and it was there that we took poor Serrallonga, fleeing the gang of savages who, unwilling to give up their prey, surrounded the carriage whistling, laughing and throwing orange peel.

On the way there, we looked at him closely; called him by his name; looked at him with cautious smiles; touched him gently on his hand and tried to get his attention in all the most agreeable ways we could think of. But everything was useless: it was as if he were blind and deaf. His vague, disorientated gaze crossed ours only once in its mysterious, fluctuating course across the earth and sky. It seemed as if the man had completely lost track of his memory, who he was and his perceptions of the world, blind and deaf to it all. It was as if his soul had left his body and had been scattered all around. What a terribly sad, mysterious, shocking thing. My God!

At first, they didn't want to let us in the aid station for dubious administrative reasons, but in the end they offered us a place to rest. There, I watched over the poor wretch until Armengol was able to come with a government decree ordering him to be provisionally detained in the poorhouse.

We then sent a telegram to his wife, who turned up devastated the next day, saying that she thought that Daniel had been at the Escobills estate where he had gone a couple of days earlier to prepare the harvest. Now, knowing how the farmer was, she suspected that this new attack of madness had come from some argument between the two. Thanks to the advice that Armengol had given her a few days before, the poor woman had come with the documents that the godless Spanish formalities required for her to arrange the incarceration of her husband. Forty-eight hours later, with all the steps and requirements formalised, Daniel was transferred to a large psychiatric ward in Horta that, for absurd reasons that escape me, was called *Paradise*.

NINE

I was stunned at the news in Armengol's letter. Not three months had passed since they had sent Daniel to the psychiatric hospital and now the poor man was dead.

I felt at once that sensation of surprise, desolation and coldness that a death so often provokes, regardless of how far removed the person was. Poor Daniel! I thought, still holding the letter in my hands. Through a sole blurry tear, it seemed as if he were right there before me, lying face up on his back and staring at the picture from the last year of university, there just two feet away from me. My enthusiastic client, my poor admirer. His whole sorry story ran through my head and my heart was in knots as I thought about how even I was on the list of accomplices to the disastrous turn of events. And there was Daniel, forgiving our jeers from prison, trusting in me when almost everybody else ignored him, and never quite finding the way or sufficient measures to show me his gratitude. My eyes welled up with the generous memories that he had left me with. My heart compelled me to go to his funeral. It was the only thing that I could do to make up for my juvenile actions in '68, and that corresponded to the friendship that the deceased had shown me. I had to honour his memory.

And in the early afternoon of that September day, I took a cab and went to pick Armengol up before we asked the driver to take us to Paradise.

Armengol was even sadder than I was. He had seen the widow and the young boy, and that picture of pain and the unexpected, brutal surprise on both of their faces had broken his heart.

'Think about it,' he said, 'those poor people heard of the death before the illness, if you can call it that in this case. The last piece of news that they had received about the patient was the report from August that they got just a few days ago in which the manager of the hospital said that Daniel was a lot more relaxed and lucid and that there was a vague hope of improving the prognosis soon. The woman had already made such an effort to have him home safe and well, despite the wholly sad and, at the same time, curious circumstances that made her effort doubly important. In these conditions, of course, news of his death without any warning has been not unlike what they describe as a sharp wake-up call.'

'Curious circumstances, you say?'

'Yes. Seeing those despicable sisters of his, who had once tried to get a judge to declare him insane, now acting as their brother's most jealous defenders, claiming that he was never mad but rather a victim of some hellish plot by his wife and her family to best use his interests as they saw fit. What's more, half of Vilaniu is out for the poor woman and her family's blood.'

'What? But have they not seen in the newspapers what the poor wretch was doing in the streets in Barcelona? Don't they say anything about the testimonies of the many doctors who, even at the aid station, considered him ill before he was sent off to the asylum? Is that not enough?'

'Don't get het up, old friend. Interests and jealousy will never be sincere. The sisters' only care is that Salomè Argila and her child have supplanted them in their brother's inheritance. The rest of them are nothing more than snakes rattling their tails so as not to be trodden on. Honestly, I don't know what it is about mental illness that makes it so mysterious, so deathly repulsive, that nobody wants to believe in or even touch it. We ourselves are proof of this.'

'It's true,' I said, thinking about our past discussions with Giberga and how long it took us to notice the madman we had before us.

'Here you have it,' added Armengol. 'Everyone understands when someone dies because of a bang on the head, meningitis or some apoplexy or head trauma, right? So why is everyone now asking how Serrallonga died, looking for the cause in another, quite different, order of illnesses, just like I'm doing now?'

'Fair enough. I, too, was going to ask how he had died.'

'Oh, all of us! We are all doing the same!'

Here we fell silent and, half dozing with the swaying of the cab, I went over and over the possible explanations. But what do I know? Do I know what he said or thought? The damned luck of the poor wretch we were going to bury weighed heavy on my heart and his sisters' monstrous conduct towards the widow had started to bother me.

We had already passed Josepets when we were overtaken by three black cabs. In one of them Armengol recognised the deceased's young son sitting next to another young man, red-faced and dressed in black, who must have been Ramon Argila, Salomè's brother.

'The widow and her father must also be in there,' said Armengol before telling the driver to get a move on up the hill.

That immensely long road of squat, new houses, perfumed gardens and large gaps overlooking the busy panorama of the hilly

Vallcarca villages rolled away before my eyes like some dead thing, annoying rather than interesting. At times it delighted me, while at others it made me sad.

We finally reached the three dirt tracks at the top of the hill and took the lone right one. All four coaches found themselves enveloped in the same cloud of dust, and fifteen minutes later we stopped in front of a tall, severe-looking iron gate.

The twenty or so of us got out of the carriages, hearing nothing but the bubbling of water from an abundantly flowing fount and the chattering of the birds sitting in the trees. After a minute's delay we walked through the gate and down a wide, tree-covered pathway before rounding a corner and going down to the right towards the edge of an English garden in front of the hospital. There was nobody else to been seen on either the pathway or in the garden and when I looked on the building itself, it sent chills through my bones. It was one of those endless, flat, symmetrical constructions with a chapel tower rising up in the middle: the men's area on one side and the women's on the other, with the same number of gates, balconies and doors. Both had been designed so that nobody could see inside and that no voice could escape through the gaps.

Armengol introduced me to the widow and her boy. When she heard my name and lifted up her eyes to look at me, doubtless in some affectionate memory, she burst into bitter tears and threw herself into her elder sister's arms, the only other woman who had accompanied her. Her father and brother approached her lovingly and, not wishing to linger in that sacred place, we disappeared into the gardens. The kiosks selling flowers and snacks, scattered around the edges of the paths like pantheons, gave the area a touch of life and we spent some moments silently walking around aimlessly, surrounded by the cemetery-like solitude. After a while we reached a large sandy terrace, surrounded by trees and rock gardens, that looked down over everything. The great peak of Tibidabo reared up before us, catching the west winds before casting its humid shadow across half of the gardens and shrouding the length of the building in darkness. The building was sunk in front of a small bare hillock which, along with other equally diminutive hills, hid Barcelona from view as if we were a thousand miles away. Looking out to the left-hand side, we could see down to the golden, sunlit plain of Horta and Sant Andreu, a collection of varied houses and criss-crossed by roads and railways. Now and again we saw steam rising from trains and heard the hustle and bustle of life below but, unintentionally, our eyes invariably fell back upon the building next to us: that sad, impenetrable, almost haunted, mysteriously dead, hospital. The lack of movement and the overbearing silence chilled our souls. Neither madmen nor wisemen were to be seen anywhere. So, what now? I wondered. Doesn't death, the absolute disappearance of someone, seemingly once ours, mean anything here? Doesn't even that disgraceful family, come to collect the remains of one who was once both their head and leader, deserve to be received by some Paradise employee other than the doorman?

From our viewpoint we could still see the little black circle of people around the widow, in the middle of the square where we had left her. They were clearly all still there due to a lack of anyone to guide them, and it made our stomachs turn. We hurried over to where they were all standing and Armengol went off to look for someone from the hospital. But rather than an official organiser or anyone of importance, it was a humble servant who proceeded to take us all over to the furthest part of the building hidden by the gardens. The servant then opened the little door to a squat, miserable structure that could well have been the coal store for the whole institute. Inside, in an open coffin sitting on a stretcher at the foot of a nondescript, candle-lit altar, we saw the body of who was once our friend, husband to the widow, and father to that pale, weak little boy who stared at him, shocked, dry-eyed and tense like someone gazing upon death's handiwork for the very first time.

That was the boy's father. He who had once adored his son and had showered him with kisses, carried him around on piggyback, bought him toys, and who had pulled that sad, sad face, hugging him as tight as possible, when he was ill. His son who he had later beaten so many times, who he had terrorised during so many nights with knife in hand, uttering those horrific cries in the alcove, guided by his lantern, the lantern that would steal the boy's breath away! Oh no! The boy had had a spectre for a father, a vision in three distinct forms: love, hate and death. And the poor boy couldn't take his eyes off that sleeping body, ruffled, immobile, buttoned up and old marble in colour. Its forehead strangely wrinkled and its glassy open eyes which, in turn, lent the corners of its lips a certain painful, bitter expression. And the boy couldn't understand why it was wearing the ashen woollen smock that he'd never seen before or why, when touched by his mother's lips as she knelt down beside it, that long, knotted hand didn't tremble or shake off its waxy colour. How well that defeated, worn out body slept.

Suddenly, behind those of us who were filling the doorway in most respectful silence, came a strange din of voices and irreverent footsteps towards us. Adela and Carolina, their eyes red like fireballs, their faces as white as sheets, were struggling to free themselves from the arms of two men holding them back. Still not quite grasping their intention, I took a reverent step backwards. But at that moment an almighty storm started all around as Ramon Argila, elbowing through the crowd, leapt into the chapel and quickly started to drag his sister away.

Oh, you madman! I thought, looking over at Daniel. What bad luck. Even in death you create nothing but trouble, arguments and insanity for your kin! As if it were contagious! But it's not your fault, you unhappy wretch. It's because of what you leave behind! But isn't this the worst indignity of all?

Young Ramon was still trying to drag his sister out of there with the best of intentions. But it was all in vain. Nothing could avoid the uproar that those contemptible sisters set about creating in there! Pushing and pulling this way and that and being the taller of the two, Adela saw the direction the widow was headed and managed to cut her off when she was only two metres from the door. Several people quickly jumped in front of her to stop her from pouncing. Others grabbed her from behind, even ripping the black veil that she wore from head to tail.

'Murderer!' she shouted, blocked off and separated from the widow. 'You poisoned my brother! Thief! Get out of here!'

The poor widow started shaking weakly and after pushing herself out of Ramon's arms fell unconscious to the floor. Her son, Nasiet, stood in front of her like a faithful dog, and her siblings and friends gathered around her to help while others tried to push away the scandalous Adela who, though removed from the area, continued to insult her. We suddenly heard a formidable crash and saw that Ramon, the widow's indignant brother, was standing in front of Adela and had slapped her hard across the face.

'Hey! Hey!' we all shouted. 'Careful! Enough! Have some respect for the dead!'

Adela's friend, Pons, then started wrestling Ramon who, like the rough and ready farmer he was, knocked him to the floor with a series of punches. Everyone else then started a terrible row around the poor widow. And it was then that the hunchback, being short in stature and therefore able to get through the crowd relatively easily, spat her poisoned sputum into the poor widow's face. But for the hunchback, penitence in Rome would have to wait: you don't get to Rome rolling around the floor as she was after the well-placed punch she got to the jaw from Argila Senior. I can still picture her there on the floor, a ball of black lace, glancing around left and right, and frothing at the mouth.

Those of us who were trying to calm the situation down and put a stop to this scandalous episode went around the room preaching peace and restraint. But nobody listened to us and not one member of the church stepped forward to impose their authority, not even to help those who needed it most. The gardens were empty, the building immutable, when the brawl suddenly burst out into the open, as if making its way into the great pantheon to that common grave of reason and sympathy. What were we seeing was so unexpected, so terrifying, so brutal that one might have thought that the Devil himself was present, like a plague infecting the reason of everyone who had set foot in those gardens. I've no idea of the absurdities that crossed my mind at that moment or my thoughts on how long it would last or how it would end.

Just at that moment a door in the garden fence was opened giving direct access to a smaller chapel. Through it, against the light of the red-hot sun and to everyone's surprise came the church's cross carried on its way to fetch the deceased. The six or seven priests following sang the *Dies irae* impassively from the other side of the wall, and this unexpected, theatrical, profoundly dramatic act scattered the brawlers, revived those lying unconscious, and quickly reminded us of the painful truth that had brought us all there.

Pons and the sisters' other friend left in embarrassment, bloodied and covered in dust, while others accompanied the terrified widow back to the carriage. Around a dozen men and I, shocked at what we had just seen, gathered behind the mourning procession made up of the boy, his grandfather and uncle. And, with silent, sad steps we followed the cross and funeral cart along the outer path, still without having seen even one member of the hospital staff. Not one of them had come to bid farewell to our friend, Daniel Serrallonga.

'As far as they're concerned, it's as if a dog had died!' I exclaimed, indignant.

'But, where do you get that idea from?' said a profoundly bitter Armengol. 'Do you really think you can find the love, charity and piety that you are looking for in a place where office workers make the rules? Order, rules, a habit of routine, and money to be made will always suffocate sympathy. This is a hospital that receives the wounded from the eternal battle. There's barely enough time to count the casualties before another arrives to occupy the still-warm bed. How very naïve you are!'

But I just bowed my head.

'God help me,' I said to myself. 'And may we be forgiven one and all.'

AUGUST, *1898*.

fə